Sun-Kissed

Sun-Kissed

LAURA FLORAND

To Melinda Utendorf

who said, "Have you ever thought about telling Mack
Corey's story?"
(and started me thinking)

And to Mia

who, when she heard that *Snow-Kissed* was the #1
short on Amazon, got huge eyes and said: "Mommy,
you should write more of those! What about *Sun-
Kissed?*"
(Next on her list of brainstorming are *Rain-Kissed*,
Storm-Kissed, and *Candy-Kissed*, but, alas, no
inspiration for those has struck yet.)
May you have twice fifty years of love, strength, and
happiness, sweetheart.

Chapter 1

Her isolation itched at him. Mack wanted to reach out and break it, like one of those damn sugar sculptures over on the bridal table, break the translucent pieces of that isolation, say, *Hey, did you notice all this world here you're missing?* He and Anne Winters had been friends—vacation house neighbors, beach walking partners—for close to twenty years, and yet she stood apart at his daughter's wedding reception, a flute of champagne in one hand, cool and distant as a queen surveying her realm.

Granted, the East Hampton beach house pretty much was her realm for the moment. Anne Winters had laid her stamp over the Corey property, turning Mack's youngest daughter's wedding into something so exquisite and protected that it made him want nothing so much as to kiss Anne's hand. *Thank you.*

Thank you for giving Jaime this, me this. This moment when we can believe nothing bad will ever touch her.

And unlike his damn French sons-in-law, he was not a hand-kisser.

He was, however, a man who had never had any qualms about treading on someone else's kingdom, taking it over, making it his. He'd gotten into such a habit of respecting Anne's, though. His most trusted ally.

As any man who ruled the world knew, trusted allies were few and far between, and a *powerful* trusted ally— well, you didn't mess with that. You were glad you had it and tried to make sure it trusted you back.

When it was attacked, you defended it, and if your defense failed—

His fist clenched by his side. Yeah, damn God. And damn the whole vicious world, for how helpless all his power had been to protect those he wanted to shield.

But that wasn't a thought for this wedding. Anne Winters had smoothed that all away, left them a space of perfect flowers, perfect tables, clever and elegant decorations, where everything was entirely beautiful. His new son-in-law's chef friends—if Dom Richard even had friends, whatever he wanted to call them—had poured into the kitchens as they got restless the day before, resulting in a rivalry to produce an ever-better tribute to the bridal couple that had been pretty damn funny and helped transform everyone's nerves into good cheer.

Even Mack's, there for a while.

There were now tables filled with their exotic and fantastical confections and chocolate sculptures on either side of the bride's head table, which had completely disturbed Anne's arrangements of classic American-style wedding cakes. Driving her crazy, of course, but she had handled it smoothly.

For them. For Jaime's sake. For his own sake, really.

He knew it was for their sake, for his, and yet there Anne stood, alone over there by an arch of pale roses, all slim elegance, with that new elf-queen cut of hers, a perfectly coiffed cap of frost blond hair, in that pale sheath dress with its delicate, shimmering hint of twilight blue. She'd only been out of prison three months—just long enough to take over Jaime's wedding and make sure it came off perfectly—and pleasure still kicked through him so intensely it was erotic to see her unbeaten, unbowed, a queen.

She was as elegant and slim and luminescent as that flute of champagne she held while she watched his oldest daughter Cade give the speech that choked herself and Jaime up and, God, him. He'd thought for a long time there that he had failed at raising two daughters who got along, but apparently that had just been teenagers. They loved each other somewhere deeper and richer than their rivalry.

Shit, Cade had been the first one to reach Jaime when she—

Yeah, *fuck*, let's not think about that now. *Think about this beautiful wedding. Think about my newest damn son-in-law.*

He walked over to Anne, and his skin settled on him like it fit again. He'd started noticing that a long time ago—how much those beach walks beside her early in the morning settled his skin. Those six months she'd been in prison, he'd only been able to get his skin to calm down again on visiting days, even though he'd wanted, every single visit, to punch his fists against the acrylic glass that separated them until the damn unbreakable thing shattered.

She looked over at him as he reached her and gave him that friendly, cool, don't-touch-me smile of hers. Shit, it got to him when she went on auto-pilot like that and included him in that smile.

"It looks beautiful," he told her, because she liked that kind of thing—courtesy. The entire foundation on which their twenty-year friendship had been constructed was just that—neighborly courtesy.

Her smile was fainter this time, still cool and distant but less a performance, more real. "Thank you. But you should be hugging Cade or something. The photographers will want to catch pictures of the bride's father in sweet moments with his daughters."

He shrugged. "Let them catch me talking to my date instead."

She gave him a wry look at being called his date, but he thought he'd been pretty clear about it, when he said, *You've got to be my date for this thing. I can't do it alone.*

That last wedding, Cade's in France last year, with all Sylvain's family stealing every atom of attention to them with their extravagant antics and skits on the bridal couple, had been—kind of crappy. To be alone that was. The wedding itself had been fun, really, and having already met his *other* future French chocolatier son-in-

3

law by then, he was more reconciled to Sylvain. But he'd missed his wife so damn bad. Having her there to see it, the way she would have beamed and gotten all misty-eyed, and...*fuck.*

Having Anne with him was a much better choice than doing that kind of thing alone. The friend who had kept him centered for the past fifteen years. Ever since Julie died, really. Or maybe he should say the past thirteen years, because for those first couple of years after the car accident, he sure as hell hadn't counted as centered, no matter how many elegant variations on comfort food Anne carried over in their exquisite packaging, in her version of caring.

She was persistent at it, caring. She wasn't *good* at it. She couldn't hug or emote like Julie had. But she kept at it. He still got elaborately packaged handmade hot chocolate mixes, complete with homemade filigree snowflake marshmallows, at Christmas, along with a perfect little card in Anne's perfect handwriting with some joke about making sure he got real chocolate. Him, the head of the largest chocolate manufacturer in the world, damn it. Just so that when he drank her stuff, he'd have that kick of amused annoyance to give it flavor.

"The last time I got caught on camera talking to you, I ended up in prison for insider trading," she said dryly.

He grunted, fresh fury rising up. It was only the five hundredth time she had made that damn joke, but she did it on purpose, some old wound she had to poke to make sure she could still treat it as funny. The memory of beating and beating at the justice system that had caught her in its clutches, that wanted to make an example of her no matter what arguments of bribery or blackmail or menace or reason he could marshal. The fucking witch-hunt. All the power in the world, and he couldn't keep the woman who had kept him sane the past fifteen years out of prison. She couldn't keep *herself* out of prison. Between them, they'd made empires worth multiple billions, and they still didn't have enough power.

4

"You have a repetitive sense of humor," he complained.

She bit back a grin, an expression that always gave him a shaft of pleasure. She wasn't, by nature, a grinner. "So you say."

He pulled her into his side with a loop of his arm, a sudden and confusing pressure of her much smaller body against his, and grinned toward the camera flash that went off. "Don't sell any shares in Corey Chocolate tomorrow," he told her as he released her.

"Fuck you," she said mildly, brushing her clothes into order as she stepped back. Ripples ran through his body from the contact. He was more than a decade past the point where he felt guilty toward Julie about all the ways he could imagine shaking Anne Winters out of her cool composure, but he still felt kind of guilty toward *Anne.*

And yet just right now he wanted to poke that guilt and rile it up. Give it something to feel guilty about. "Aww, you looked cute in orange." He grinned at her.

She'd looked *arrogant.* She'd looked like a Lady Godiva who didn't need the damn hair. She'd walked into that visiting room in those damn orange pajamas every time the same way she'd walked into the courtroom in those high-heeled pumps and those perfect skirts and with that *fuck you* cool tilt of her chin. The one that had not endeared her to the jury at all. And she'd crossed her legs and thought *fuck you* straight at them when she realized it, too.

She gave him that same cool, *fuck you* look right now. But her mouth curved wryly.

Humor. Sometimes it was the only way you could bump fists with someone across a whole dump truck load of shit.

"Pay attention to your daughters," she told him. "Cade spent a lot of time on this slideshow for her sister."

All the lights in the gardens dimmed, all at once, to allow the images to show on the white screen set up on the far side of the dance floor and all the flower-decked tables around it.

Mack turned his head as the first image flashed—Jaime as a newborn, so small he used to hold her in one hand, oh fuck. And then all grinning and chubby-cheeked and freckled and smeared with chocolate at one of their production facilities. There was one with Julie, helping her learn how to walk, Jaime's little one-year-old round face just as proud as punch in herself, and Julie beaming, her red head bent to Jaime's baby-pale red-gold hair. His throat clogged. There were both his little girls, peeking out of some giant resin dinosaur egg in a museum, when they were, what, two and five? So freaking innocent, so sweet. The way they used to pile up on him in the morning. He used to get up extra early, try to sneak in some work while Julie and the girls were sleeping, so he could take his time over breakfast with them all, so he could get home a little early and not work again until after they went to bed. It had succeeded—poorly, at that age. They seemed to have a radar for when he woke up, and no matter how early it was, five minutes later, there would be some small, sleep-mussed head poking in through his office door. Then the run, run across the still-dark office that kind of scared them, even though he had learned to keep nightlights along the hall, and the little body burying itself in his arms, snuggling up. Falling back to sleep *just* at that angle where he couldn't actually use his arms and get any work done, but—he'd liked it too much to give it up.

More photos with Julie. There she was fixing Jaime's hair. Holding the hands of both girls in their extra-fancy sparkly dresses as they tried to wear their mother's heels. Julie's old charm bracelet showed on her wrist, the one with the precious stones for him and for each of their girls, the one she'd worn right up until the day she died. Mack had given it to Jaime for her "something old".

Cade had tried to bring in, through photos, all those things Julie would have liked to do with her daughter at her wedding—fix hair, help with her pretty dress, smile proudly and tenderly as Jaime set off on her next phase in life.

Photos with him. Lots with him, lifting them up in the air, twirling them around, playing with them in the waves here. Christ, had he really looked that young when they were babies? He was just a kid himself, and already thinking he could run the world? Never lacked for nerve, had he?

A beautiful family photo, one of the many that decorated their house, he and Julie each with an arm around each other, the other arm cradling the girls into the shelter of their happy family.

A newspaper headline from that time Jaime had gotten arrested at a G8 summit, a freckle-faced nineteen-year-old. God almighty, that girl had been a handful. Some photos of her with a bouncy red-gold ponytail on cocoa farms, a delicate photographic balancing act on Cade's part, to honor that phase of her life without letting it lead them too close to another transformative event in Jaime's life, one that Mack still couldn't think about without his breath shortening, his body caving, as if fists were pounding his lungs. Without his own fists clenching and punching until they broke things.

He glanced at Dom, the big, rough, black-haired Parisian chocolatier Jaime had chosen for herself. Not exactly his dream son-in-law, but Mack had to give him credit—the man would take care of her. He would fight for her. Fight *him* for her, the bastard. Not that many men willing to fight *him.* Dom would do his damn best by her.

Another photo, just of Julie, a beautiful one where the sunlight fell on her face just right and her expression as she looked into the camera was so tender, so loving. Under it, Cade had captioned *I am so proud of you.*

At the head table, Jaime bent her head and started to cry.

Mack took a step forward—but Dom's hand was already there. Curving over the nape of her neck. Big and scarred and saying, *It's all right. Cry if you need to. I'm here.*

Dom was there. Not Mack. She had somebody else to hug her now, when she needed it, whose hugs she would want more than her daddy's.

The last slide came up, Jaime and Dom in their wedding clothes just outside the church only an hour ago, Jaime's head tilted up, Dom's tilted down, the expression on their faces—

A hand took his arm, pulling him gently around.

"Damn." He scrubbed the back of his hand across his eyes, breathing raggedly.

Anne kept tugging, guiding him away from the crowd, through an arch of roses to a private spot on the veranda wrapping around the side of the house. It was a lovely night, the lights that wove through the garden glowing warm gold again post-slideshow, the band shifting, getting ready for the first dance. He'd have to get back. He had to do the daddy-daughter dance.

Oh, fuck.

Shit, and he'd been the man who once thought he was too tough to cry. Before his daughters and his wife pummeled all his emotions wide open. He scrubbed water off his face again, trying to calm his stupid, ragged breathing.

"Sorry," he told Anne, who probably *never* cried. She probably hadn't even let herself cry the night before she went to *prison.* "Damn. It's just that she's—he's—oh, damn, they're all gone now. They're not my little girls."

Anne stroked the flower petals of his boutonnière, the one she had made for him, as if getting those petals to lie exactly right would fix everything. "They're still your little girls," she said quietly.

"They are to *me*," he agreed, anguished. "But they're not to anyone *else*. No one will ever, ever love them as much as I—" He broke off, sniffling like an idiot, turning his head to stare at the ocean across the dune.

"I know," Anne said, wistfulness shifting across her face, so subtly he was probably the only man who would ever spot it. And it had taken him fifteen years of walks along the beach. Her only son was married, too, although Mack remembered the rough spot that marriage had gone through, remembered a year and a half when he hadn't seen Kai at all and Kurt had been a mess, as if the younger man was being oh-so-slowly stretched on a rack, inch by excruciating inch past bearing.

And if Mack remembered it, Kurt's mother was most certainly remembering it, too. The goddamn agony of seeing your child hurt and not being able to stop it.

He pulled Anne into his arms, suddenly, knowing she wouldn't like it, but just needing a shared hug, for a moment, with someone who really did understand.

Her body went startled and stiff in his arms, which pissed him off somehow, and he snuggled it, teaching her body how well they fit. He'd had a wife and two girls, and he knew how well a hug fit. She relaxed so warily you'd think he'd been asking a snowman to sunbathe, honest to God.

It's not going to kill you, damn it. You're not actually made of frozen water.

Snow Queen, they'd always called her in the press during that enraging criminal justice pursuit. Or Ice Queen. For the woman who compulsively collected houses and turned them into homes. Yeah, get a mass of people yapping at you and they were always idiots.

She stood very still in his arms, like she was pretty sure she was *not* the right puzzle piece for this spot.

Jesus, Anne. He leaned back against the railing, putting some stubbornness in this hug now, pulling her in tight. God, a hug felt good. Even a hug whose smaller half wasn't quite sure it wanted to be part of it. He'd just been hugging Jaime before he walked her down the aisle only an hour ago, so it wasn't as if he didn't have hugs in his life, and yet a hug that wasn't father-daughter but was, you know, man-woman...

Felt good.

Felt damn *alive.*

Over Anne's blond pixie cut, through the roses, he saw Dom pull Jaime onto the dance floor, that big, rough, aggressive, utterly enamored son-of-a-bitch handling his daughter, pulling her in close, the strains of the slow dance reaching them on the veranda gently. Jaime laid her head against Dom's tux with so much trust, as if she was letting herself completely go.

The way she used to lay her head against *Mack's* chest when she was a little girl, and *fuck you, Dom. Why do they grow up? How did I lose that?*

His arms squeezed Anne harder, holding on to the only thing he could.

But Dom knew what a precious thing he had. Mack had to give him that, even though it made him want to punch the man in jealousy. Jealousy that surged higher as Dom's head bent to Jaime, as he held her close. Everything about big, bad Dom Richard was on display right there, for all those camera-happy wedding guests and the professional team, flashes going off everywhere. The man was ripped-open, raw, exposed. Vulnerable and trying to be strong.

Cade and Sylvain got up and moved out onto the floor, even though Mack was pretty sure they weren't supposed to do that—wasn't the first dance just supposed to be the bridal couple? Trust Sylvain to want to steal the spotlight.

But then Luc and Summer got up, Summer gently pregnant. A distant cousin to his own daughters, Summer had spent a fair amount of time visiting his girls as a child, mostly because Julie loathed Summer's parents, Sam and Mai Corey, and tried to rescue Summer whenever she could. Sam had multiple estates in the Hamptons, and had never bothered to make a home out of a single one of them. So despite their other options, Mack was putting Luc and Summer up in one of the guest bedrooms here, along with what seemed like half of France at this point.

More of those chef buddy-enemies of Dom's got up and joined the dancers—a blond surfer one with a date who looked part Asian and that big tawny guy with a small woman in very high heels. They all drifted into a loose circle around the central couple.

They were shielding the bride and groom, Mack finally realized. Spreading out around Jaime and Dom, probably driving the photographers crazy, but breaking up the intensity of focus on that raw, exposed tenderness.

That was…kind of good to know, that his son-in-law had enemies like that. They were way better than most of the people who tried to claim they were Mack's friends. Since Jaime had already done the deed and married Dom, it was good to know the two of them had backup.

He turned Anne in his arms so that her back was to his chest, stubborn about not letting her go, now that he had violated twenty years of non-touching. Might as well go for broke, as he usually thought about things he wanted. "Look," he told her. "Kurt and Kai look happy."

Kurt had been coming over to play at the Corey house since before Julie died. Mack had bought the Corey beach house when Julie first got pregnant, partly because the cocoa scents that permeated their hometown of Corey made her so sick. He'd chosen the Hamptons because it was close enough to New York and attracted enough movers and shakers on "vacation" themselves, that, like them, he could manage that ambitious over-achiever's juggling act—giving his kids a special summer at the beach, in which he actually participated as much as he could, while still continuing to get things done. The fact that he'd bought it so early in his climb, when Corey was worth a couple hundred million not multiple billions, meant that its ten thousand square feet on a three-acre beachfront lot were modest compared to some of the estates on this beach. For his kids, it had become that place where everything fun and carefree happened. Maybe that sense of happiness and time with family was why Jaime had wanted to have her wedding here rather than at the Corey estate back in the town that was named for them.

Anne had bought the place next door shortly after her divorce, just over twenty years ago. Her fortune had still been counted in the tens of millions back then, too, her star rising fast but her own expertise at how to manage that rise not yet at its fullest. In the parlance of East Hampton, her three-story home was a "cottage", and Anne, of course, had turned it into the most perfect, welcoming, fairytale setting for herself and her son. Not about to let the utter failure of her marriage destroy her ability to make herself and her son a *home*.

Kurt, twelve or thirteen when they moved in, had been the lonely kid next door whom Julie had welcomed easily into their play on the beach, and of course Cade and Jaime had *loved* having the older boy play with them. They'd hero-worshipped him as little girls building sandcastles, because he built amazing sandcastles, as if Anne had personally trained him so she could put his sandcastles on the cover of her magazine. Kind of proved how lonely he was, that he'd latched onto the girls in return, not such a common thing for a boy just becoming a teenager to be so happy to play with girls five and eight years old.

Now he didn't look lonely anymore. Or he did, in a way, as he and his wife Kai joined the other couples on the dance floor in the middle of the gardens—intensely alone in each other, as if each other was all the world need hold. In Mack's early days with Julie, the two of them had felt like that, before they had kids and "only each other" seemed a small thing.

And now the kids were gone. All that size of him— wife, kids—reduced all the way back to one.

He felt too big for himself. Like he couldn't *be* that single, stingy number again.

Anne sighed a little, and her weight actually settled for a second back against him, surprising him. Surprising his *groin*, which hadn't been nearly optimistic enough to anticipate her butt nestling against it. Her arms came up to fold over his arms, wrapped over her middle. Maybe Anne had had too much champagne. "They do look happy, don't they?"

He angled his head, trying to see her face, but she'd always been a hard read. Wistfulness? Relief? One of those weird combinations of both, not unlike his when he looked at his kids with their husbands?

He squeezed her a little. *I understand.*

Nice to have that. A physical exchange of understanding.

"Kai seems to be surviving Summer," Anne said unexpectedly, and one of her slim, strong hands tightened over his forearm.

"Kai and Summer don't get along?" It always surprised him how much women disliked Summer. She was such a pretty, sweet little thing. Always had been, even as a kid, even when his own girls were squabbling all over the lawn about some anthill or God knew what.

He was sure as hell glad his own daughters hadn't gone through as many boyfriends as Summer had later, though, because it would have driven him completely insane. He'd far rather they squabble and stand up for themselves than think they had to please half the men on the face of the planet.

Anne's head shook, the back of it rubbing against his chest. This was starting to feel too good. Much too good. He'd had so many damn fantasies about Anne, because it had been so safe. There was that sheet of glass between them, and it wasn't as if she was going to *know* what was going on in the privacy of his bedroom. And the fact that he felt a little guilty about it, invading her in his sex dreams, only added that kinky twist of pleasure to it. Made it hotter.

But actually touching her like this had his body all confused. So used to taking her over in his head and doing whatever the hell he wanted and always having the Ice Queen melt, every single way and time, that his hand just kept thinking it could run right down under the band of her skirt and slip a finger where it made her moan, or run up to pinch her nipples and have *that* make her moan. His brain just kept *going* with the fantasy, so used to the easy, private pleasure of it that it slid right down that path with delighted eagerness.

To where she parted her legs and begged. To where she said, *Yeah, fuck me,* with that cool, enigmatic smile of hers, and he damn well *did.*

Shit, now he wished she'd stiffen up and pull her butt back off his groin. Because otherwise—well, she wasn't an idiot, Anne Winters.

She'd conceived a child, so she had to know what an erect penis felt like. As counter-intuitive as it seemed with her, as convinced a man could get that she only had sex in his own dirty little mind.

Anne drew a breath and sighed it out, a soft, vulnerable sound. That was—odd. Anne didn't *do* vulnerable. She looked at a jury and thought, *If I play all fragile, I bet they'll let me off,* and instead of *doing that,* she gazed them straight in the eyes and thought, *Fuck you.* The admiration Mack had felt watching her, and the impotent fury at the damn Department of Justice, had caught him in a tight fist and *held him.* Held him every damn day she was in prison. Still held him.

"Kai had some miscarriages," Anne said very low. Her hand flexed again on his wrist. Made his wrist feel damn strong. Nice to be the wrist that could offer a hand that capable all the resistance it needed when it wanted to squeeze something.

Mack gazed blankly at Anne's daughter-in-law, his mind more and more on the feel of his wrist, the feel of his groin, having trouble with the conversation. "And that makes her not like Summer?" What *was* it with women and Summer? Were that many women that freaking insecure? He didn't go around hating better-looking men.

"Mack." Anne's voice was quiet, and a little stern. *Pay attention. Use your head.* She didn't indulge much idiocy, Anne. When your decisions affected half the world and, more importantly, your kids, it was incredibly helpful to have someone in your camp who wouldn't let you be an idiot. "Look at Summer."

"She seems happy?" he said tentatively. Happy. Sure that she was loved. Relaxed into it, golden-haired and luminous with contentment. Did even *Anne* hate the thought of Summer being happy? He'd thought she was stronger than that.

"She looks like a Madonna," Anne said, with an undertone of—something. Something dark.

When he thought of Madonnas, he thought of Renaissance paintings in museums to which he had kept dragging the girls because he was so sure their mother would have done it had she still been around. But—oh. The belly. "It's...sweet?" He didn't know why the hell he should have to feel so dubious about this, like maybe a beautiful, happy pregnant young woman *wasn't* sweet to his conversational partner. Women were weird about each other sometimes.

"Yes." Anne sounded quiet and dark, like someone who wanted to curl up alone and get some sleep. "But Kai might find that painful."

It still took him a minute. And then—

Oh.

Oh.

That had never even occurred to him before. Women didn't get over that kind of thing?

He looked at Kurt, the long, lean, intelligent, careful man he had once imagined might become his son-in-law, now holding his wife as if they were the only two in the world. As if he could *make* them be the only two in the world. They danced within their own precious bubble, his brown head bent to hers, his back always, always blocking Summer from Kai's view and from his, too, Kai's blond head resting against his tux, her face at ease, quiet, absorbed in him, as soft and dreaming as a dapple of sunlight through the leaves.

15

"Your son's a good man," Mack said suddenly, bluntly. He figured Anne would want to know.

"He is, isn't he?" She sounded as if the awareness had snuck up on her and caught her in some painful grip of too much pride. Yeah. His pride in his daughters did that kind of thing to him, too, at the trickiest moments. "He turned out so much better than his father," she added low.

"Well, shit, of course," Mack said involuntarily. "With you for a mother?"

Anne looked up at him at that, startled and caught, eyes fixed on him as if he'd said something amazing. She had eyes like honey on moss, this elusive hint of green and sunlight, like catching sight of something magical deep in a forest just as it ducked away.

"No offense, Anne, but you married a fucking weakling the first time around." Not at all the kind of guy who could face down whatever bad happened to him and tell it, *Fuck you.*

"The first time?" she said quizzically, which was just one of those things she did, split hairs in an ironic way to hide her emotional reactions.

Yes, he knew she'd only been married once so far. Did she expect him to say her life was over halfway through? "Pick someone with guts the next time around," he ordered her bluntly, mostly because he liked the way her eyes narrowed at him when he tried to boss her around like he bossed the rest of the world.

They did narrow, kicking a charge right through him, making his stupid body drag him straight back to another fantasy, this one where she gave him that *make me* look, and, because it was a *fantasy, you stupid body, not real,* he *did.* He made her do all kinds of things, in all kinds of positions. And she came in every single one of them, of course.

He took a breath, trying to squeeze his hips back away from her, but his butt was already resting on the railing. Just then the door onto the veranda opened, and the wedding circus master pushed her head out and beckoned frantically. "You're on in just a minute! The song is almost over!"

Oh, shit. He was still aroused.

And it was the daddy-daughter dance!

Fuck.

He shoved Anne away from him, then made sure to steady her on her feet. "You stay away from me," he told her sternly, just to be on the safe side. He knew damn well if he gave her an order she would ignore it, and he didn't want her shutting him out for the rest of the night in overreaction to a penis or anything.

Then he strode to the other end of the veranda, nearest the closest bathroom, and snatched a glass of ice water off the tray of a waiter as he passed.

In the bathroom, he jerked his pants off, stood over the toilet, and hesitated a long second, grimacing. There were other ways to get rid of this thing, but—shit. He was not jerking off in a bathroom at his daughter's wedding. Screwing up his eyes tight and turning his head away— he dashed the ice water over himself.

Aaaagh.

That—that—*shit.*

He grabbed a towel and more or less smacked himself dry—afraid to rub—and then jerked his pants back on.

And went out to dance with his daughter on her wedding day like a normal man.

Chapter 2

"What's wrong?" Anne's son asked, sliding into the chair beside her. Anne had just finished straightening its sea-green bow and was automatically adjusting the flower arrangement in the middle of the table to make up for a bloom some guest had stolen to wear in his hair a little earlier. Some of their guests were beginning to get in quite the liquored-up, merry mood. "You look worried."

In public? With cameras to catch it? She smoothed her expression immediately. *You want to see me sweat, world? Come to the gym.*

You'll find me in the boxing ring, pretending my trainer's headgear is your head.

"Something wrong with the wedding cake?" Kurt guessed wryly.

Her son was so aggravating sometimes. She loved him, but he just put her in the *mom* category and dismissed it at that. On the other hand, she could hardly say, *No, there was a demanding penis just pressed up against my butt and my butt still feels...odd.*

Then again...she'd built an empire out of herself worth nearly a billion dollars while she was a divorced single mom. She was a convicted felon. Maybe she could say whatever the hell she wanted. "Well, if you look at the back side of that blue one, there's a finger print where I couldn't resist a taste of the frosting, but maybe no one will notice."

Kurt gave her a perplexed look. The odds of Anne Winters sneaking frosting or allowing even a hair fine imperfection in anything she did were approximately 998,547,321 million to one. Her current net worth, according to Forbes, but Jesus, what did those guys have? Hackers on all her accounts?

"Lighten up, Kurt," she said, and took a sip of her champagne.

Kurt blinked. His eyebrows went up. "Prison had a very unexpected effect on you."

She shrugged, wishing for a cigar she could bite the tip off of and drive him completely insane, or at least for the ability to *slouch* in her chair, but her spine just didn't seem to work that way. "You're a corporate lawyer." He negotiated the hell out of her company's contracts for her. Brilliant, her son, almost mercilessly so in certain circumstances. Those precise, contract-negotiation circumstances when he could hide his sensitive heart. "Since when are you familiar with the expected effects of prison?"

Kurt narrowed his eyes just a little. He had hazel eyes from his father, but so much more beautiful. The way they would look up at her when he was little, so sincere and determined. Brown hair from his father. But a heart and a strength nothing like his father's. She hadn't needed Mack to tell her that he had turned out better than Clark.

Despite her, probably, but some days she was determined to take some credit.

Kai laughed from the other side of him at the round table. The sound felt strange against Anne's skin, like an unexpected cascade of warm water when she had thought everything frozen. When part of her wanted to insist everything was *supposed* to be frozen, wasn't it? It had been frozen for her.

She had vomited in terror, the night before she had to surrender herself to prison. The first time she had let anything get to her like that in twenty years, but alone in her room, she hadn't been able to stop. Still, even then she'd known that she wouldn't have any trouble with at least one of those prison tips she had found online: never, ever show them anything you really feel, not fear, not weakness, not joy. It could all be used against you. She'd gotten that part down so very long ago, layer after frozen layer separating herself from the world's power to hurt her, accumulated year after year as she kept doing it, as no one every broke through.

But prison had weakened something in her. She knew it had. Because now some other part of her melted under Kai's laughter, surging up in this sudden geyser of grief for herself and hope for them: *God, if my son could have that happiness, that love, that support for his whole life. If he could get to keep it. Even when things get bad.*

That laughter of Kai's. That laughter that Anne had never really known how to give him, when he needed it, that had made his choice of wife such a cruel slap as she realized: *Oh. All those things I tried to teach him—self-control, and persistence, and calm, and being strong enough to count only on yourself—he went and found the exact opposite. As if nothing I gave him was what he needed at all.*

But now—she looked across the table at Kai. Their eyes met, and something passed from Kai to her, this quiet, a gentleness in her brown eyes that was almost tender. Anne couldn't fathom it.

Almost nobody showed Anne gentleness, or quiet, or tenderness. Her quiet came from herself, from when she sank into her work. Sometimes, during that period when he was separated from Kai, Kurt would come by, bringing with him a precious, uncommon quiet, a quiet that was shared. They would talk in a way they never could when he was a teenager, and each read a book for a while, or play chess. Sometimes he would even, with a wry look, help her with her crafts, the way he used to when he was a child before he rebelled into all those boyish sports. He would concentrate on those crafts as if they were a lifeline, and her heart would go out to him: *Oh, God, Kurt, please don't turn out like me.*

It had been a strange mix of good and bad, that time. Her son with her again, needing her, the two of them understanding each other perhaps more than they ever had. But only because he was so profoundly unhappy.

Kai had saved Kurt from that unhappiness in the end, not Anne. Or Kurt had saved Kai. Or maybe both together, maybe that was the secret, that they had somehow managed that meshing of souls and hearts, that strange word *together* which had shattered for her so long ago and hurt so much in its breaking that she'd kept all her walls up ever since to protect herself from accidentally letting her heart mesh with someone else's again.

She frowned suddenly and turned her head to look at Mack. Even without his daughter's bridal gown to draw the eye, he was easy to spot. He always carried himself as if he owned every room he was in or would own that room in two minutes if he decided it was worth his effort. Which was a very accurate self-assessment on his part.

Both his sons-in-law were taller than he was, but he had a heft to his shoulders and a lean, athletic way of moving that made him seem like a mastiff, or an alpha wolf. Someone ready to take out the jugular of anyone who threatened his hold on the world, definitely. Or of anyone who threatened his family, because to him it was the same thing. His hold on the world was *for* his family, just Mack's way of giving his all to keep them strong and safe.

The perfectly tailored tux gave him a civilized coating—Mack knew entirely how to be civilized—but it was just a coating. The gray hair and the lines at the corners of his eyes added to his presence, made him far more compelling even than he had been as the smoother thirty-three year old she had first met. Those lines just proved how experienced he was in wielding power, in fighting off all attackers, taking them out, and then expanding his hold where once those attackers had been.

Right now he had one arm around his freckled, red-haired daughter, the other holding her hand, as they danced in some loose approximation of the waltz. Mack was an excellent dancer, but at the moment he seemed to be seeking more a very long hug. In her slim, simple white silk, Jaime looked innocent and young against her father's bigger body and black tux, her face tilted up to him, beaming with happiness and hope, and Anne's heart relaxed a little.

She liked knowing she had helped give Jaime and Mack this moment. Every perfect line of wedding decorations that framed father and daughter and the bridal couple, every element capturing that moment and holding it as exquisitely as Anne could. Because Anne knew what the definition of *moment* was.

And she wanted something longer for Mack's children, as she did for her own son and daughter-in-law.

Homes that lasted, that held their perfect happy lives forever.

And when those lives couldn't be perfect, she still wanted those homes to hold them, to shelter them as best a home could, until they could reach peace and maybe even happiness again. She glanced back at her son and Kai.

And her heart relaxed a little more. Yes. There was peace and happiness in her son's strong hand curving gently over his wife's, in that little sigh of trust that ran through Kai as her body relaxed so close to his.

A ghost of envy touched Anne again, this cool, supercilious finger of it that liked to sneak its way into her life and stroke her possessively even while she told it to fuck off. Envy was a sexual harasser, the bastard, and Anne had never been the type to put up with that shit. But envy kept trying anyway.

I'm not envious, I'm curious, she told the wormy little pervert coolly. *How do women manage that? That's all I want to know.* All those women, so relaxed and trusting, all around her: Jaime with her father and with her new husband, Kai with Kurt, Cade with Sylvain, Summer with Luc Leroi, all those other chef-friend-couples of theirs. Even the ones busy sparring and laughing while they danced, like Philippe and Magalie over there, seemed to be doing it from a position of complete trust.

How? How do you trust that way? How do you relax?

And oddly, despite the ocean's distance across the dune, the sound of waves filled her, the scent of sea, the yield of sand under her feet, and the cool breeze off the ocean as the light eased its shimmer over the horizon, stretching across the water to her. With that scent of sea came a solid body walking beside her. No scent to him, because the sea wind stripped away all scents but its own. Often no real shape, because some mornings they walked and walked without her ever turning her head, both their gazes on the waves and the sand. A strong, deep male voice, using her as a sounding board as he worked his way through decisions that made most other men prefer to be anything, anyone rather than the person with whom the buck stopped.

A man once, who had fallen to his knees in the sand and clawed up chunks of it that he threw into the water, threw and threw, beating himself against sand while he sobbed, his face red with rage and pain, after Jaime had been found beaten in Côte d'Ivoire and airlifted out.

Anne hadn't had the slightest idea what to do. You couldn't calm that pain or tell it to go away. He needed to throw sand at the sea and weep and rage. So she'd just sat on the sand beside him, so that she wasn't looking down at his helpless rage from some position of superiority, and lifted her own handful of sand over and over, squeezing it, watching it trickle away from her fingers, waiting. When he'd finally calmed, she'd reached out a hand and closed it over his. He'd sniffled helplessly and lifted their joined hands to cover his eyes, just staying there, bowed, exhausted with rage and grief, for ages.

Yeah, she was pathetic. The man's daughter had been beaten within an inch of her life, and the best Anne could manage was to sit beside him on the sand and touch his hand. Well, and she'd baked Jaime one hell of a lot of cookies.

"You two need to go back on your trip around the world," she told her son and daughter-in-law.

Sometimes, in secret in her head, she liked to skip that awkward "son and daughter-in-law" phrasing and just call them her children. Pretend her son had brought her that daughter she'd always wanted back in the day when that want had been so important to her that she'd let its unfulfillment break her whole world. "Weren't you going to spend a year?"

"The last time I tried to leave you alone, you got arrested for insider trading," Kurt said.

Anne frowned at him. How had that kid grown up with such a gift for modulated irony? "You could hardly have stopped it."

"I could probably have advised you not to *do* it, if I'd been aware."

"Advised me not to be seen talking with people and then making business decisions the next day based on what I picked up in the conversations?" Anne asked dryly. *Thanks, kid. How* did *I build a billion-dollar empire without you?*

"Advised you not to mislead investigators about it, at least."

It had been what she'd actually gotten convicted on. "They were being nosy," Anne said. "And pissing me the hell off."

Kurt opened a hand. "Thus the usefulness of a lawyer."

Anne's mouth curved in a smile, despite the best she could do to press it down. She did like her son. Obviously, she loved him, but she *liked* him, too, that wry, firm way he stood up to her and still loved her, even though she was apparently so far from his ideal of womanhood that he'd sought out her exact opposite as his wife. "Go to Cambodia or something, Kurt. Didn't you two say you wanted to see Angkor?"

They'd only been gone a month on their trip around the world before her arrest and the whole trial mess started, and then the trial had dragged on *forever*. Until her empire had fallen under that billion-dollar mark as her stock deteriorated in all the uncertainty, and Anne had realized it would be better for her company to quit fighting and get it over with.

But all through the trial, she'd at least been able to see Kurt and Kai were back *together*. After that terrible rift between them, as if they were ice floes sundered and drifting apart over Arctic water, they now seemed to be a whole of two again and kissed by the sun. It had been a knowledge to take with her into the courtroom every day, and later to carry in a snug knot inside her in prison: *Whatever shit I have to deal with, at least my son is happy. So...Fuck. You.*

"I've been out three months," she added, dryly. It didn't seem that long to her. Sometimes it felt as if she'd just barely escaped from the Gates of Hell. But she refused to look back. No point getting turned into a pillar of salt. "We've established that I'm not going to have a nervous breakdown, right? Go ahead and go."

"Maybe we will," Kurt said and tightened his hand just a little on Kai's. Kai jerked her gaze back from Summer's gently rounded belly and smiled at Kurt, nodding.

Kurt lifted her hand and kissed it, which made Anne bite back another grin. These French chefs were starting to infect the whole place.

If Mack Corey kissed *her* hand next, she'd know it was an unstoppable plague.

He'd damn well better not do that. A poky penis was one thing, but hand-kissing—they'd been allies and friends for at least fifteen years. Twenty, if you counted the neighborly relationship that had started before Julie's death. Sexual arousal was manageable. In fact, the thought of that sexual arousal still had all kinds of little private muscles squeezing in this achy, restless way. But tenderness—the very idea of it made her lungs feel ragged and shaky, as if air was just whistling through their perforations and leaving them agonizingly empty.

"I'll give you twenty-four hours to pick your own next destination, and if not, I'm buying you tickets," she told her...children and stood, desperate to shake off that ragged feeling.

Kai bumped Kurt's knee, and Kurt glanced from her to Anne. "Want to dance?" he asked his mother.

Anne stilled. It was a nice thought on Kai's part, but she wasn't entirely sure she did. Those quiet, stolen moments with Kurt as an adult weren't hers. They could never be hers. He had moved on. Anne was alone, that thing she had prepared herself to be, taught herself to be, from the time Kurt's father had first divorced her.

But...she looked at her tall, lean son. She was so damn proud of him. "You don't mind if I steal him?" she asked Kai.

Kai smiled and shook her head gently. "You didn't mind when I stole him from you."

Anne looked at her blankly. "Yes, I did." Kids. They could be so oblivious sometimes.

"Flattered as I am by this notion of ownership, can I mention I'm a grown man?" Kurt asked the world at large. But Anne noticed that he squeezed *Kai*'s hand, letting her know that he did, in fact, belong to *her.*

Damn it, letting go of kids was hard.

Sometimes she still wondered if she would have done at all better at it if she'd had a couple more to spread the love around, as she'd wanted.

"Come on, Mom," Kurt said, and pulled her onto the dance floor.

Her shoulders relaxed involuntarily as she looked up at him. They had to, for the dance position, as he put a hand at the small of her back and took her other hand. Her tall son. She could still remember him learning how to dance, and that weird shift in power when he learned to lead properly—when he got to guide *her.* Dictate *her* steps.

He still had the most beautiful hazel eyes the world had ever made. For a long time she'd been afraid only she would ever understand how precious those hazel eyes were, but her daughter-in-law had figured it out.

She smiled up at him, happy. Increasingly happy with this moment, the way her careful construction of physical beauty in table settings and candles and party favors and flowers now sheltered so much genuine happiness. Sometimes happiness that had been picked back up and put together out of ruins. Sometimes happiness just starting to bloom. The range of it, from new and innocent, to old and tried and wiser, nourished the hope that her son would be okay. Kai would be okay. Jaime and Dom would be okay. They would be happy.

Happy together.

That alien, taunting word.

Chapter 3

"I see you let *him* lead," Mack complained good-naturedly. His stride seemed to eat up the space between them. It always did, especially, somehow, when he headed toward her.

He'd just finished dancing with Cade. Jaime was just leaving the floor with her grandfather, James Corey, or Jack, as he preferred to be called, eighty-four and still driving Mack as crazy as ever. Anne had been averting a catering disaster. The wedding organizer had only considered it a minor malfunction, which still had Anne's nerves strung a little tight. If Anne hadn't been on her, the organizer might not even have bothered *correcting* it.

Mack's approach buffeted power against her perimeter, as it always did. That man was a walking power source. He had ruled the world most of his life, so he knew you could never take ruling the world for granted. You had to keep your mind on it. Otherwise the world would buck up and throw you the hell off.

Rebellious and ungrateful and wriggly in the hands of its masters and often ugly, that world. Unless Anne smoothed it out. Anne turned the world into something beautiful and made at least some part of it desperately grateful for that beautification, too. She showed them how to paint their tomato posts blue or put their dishwashing liquid in elegant old bottles or frost a cake like a professional or unstick an old drawer, and they said, *Thank you, for turning us into something we can manage.*

Mack carried the power in his shoulders, in the long strides of a man who walked and ran and swam his worries off, who beat them into submission via a game of squash, who took half his meetings out onto a golf course. A tux looked good on him, but she liked him better in the jeans and T-shirt he wore on the beach early in the morning, that look that said *I am not working, I am being me,* that look she was one of the few people to see. That look when the corners of his eyes relaxed, and his lips softened, so that you could see the fine lines left by years of tension and determination through the peace in his face.

"I try to let you lead," Anne told him sweetly. "Apparently you just don't know how to take charge." She smiled a bit, and the man who liked to take charge of half the world responded to the challenge instantly.

"I'm holding myself back," he retorted. "Don't know if you can stand me at full power."

Anne's spine stiffened, her eyes narrowing a little. "You think there's something you can throw at me that I can't take?"

"Yeah." Mack waited just long enough for her to simmer and held her eyes. "Me."

"Really." All her belly muscles went taut, in a happy way, her core bracing for a challenge. Her fingers itched for her boxing gloves. "You want to try me, Mack Corey?"

His smile was sharp and predatory. "Yes. In fact."

Her mouth went dry, for no reason she could understand. Something *alive* surged through her, so alive she didn't know what to do with it. Her hands flexed. "I'll go as many rounds with you as you care to name."

"You know, I always thought you would, Anne." He leaned into her, and just like that, twenty years as neighbors and friends got shifted to another angle—that of a man's big body leaning over a smaller woman's, one forearm bracing against the tree. "But I'm not planning on boxing."

Her heart started to pound so hard it was like that one last minute before she walked out of prison into the flash of cameras everywhere. How had their whole world just tilted this way? Had the last child to leave their friendship-joined nests left them that off-balance? "Good," she managed, looking him in the eye. Because this was the man who had taught her that—how to look a jury in the eye and think *fuck you* and not back down. She'd honed it through twenty years of looking him in the eye and holding her own. "Because I'd wipe the floor with you."

"The floor's for teenagers. They're always in too much of a hurry to get things right. A bed now, or a table, or a counter—a man can do something with that."

Her lips parted on the punch of breath that went through her. If they were boxing, then that blow had snuck right in under her guard and gotten her in the gut. "Are you drunk?"

"See." His grin grew sharper, victorious and angry both. "You're already ducking and weaving."

"That's because I'm getting in a position to punch your head right off. Are you sure you want to mess with me without putting on headgear?"

"Are you sure you're not going to call foul and leap right out of the ring?"

So much energy zinged through her, it was as if long-amputated nerve endings had suddenly received some drug injection and reconstituted themselves. Sensitive and burning. She wanted to itch at them, or at the very least rub her arms, but she wouldn't give him the victory. "I can't believe you're going to ruin a twenty-year friendship because you got drunk and horny."

"I can't believe it either," he said, and his other arm came up, so that now he had her entirely caged, like those damn French chefs liked to do when they were flirting with their girlfriends or wives. Which they seemed to do every single second they weren't messing up her wedding cake arrangements. "Our friendship isn't that goddamn weak."

She drew a breath that came out almost on a laugh. Because, well—it *wasn't*. She could haul off and slap him right now, and he'd still be on that beach tomorrow morning. He'd still text her ten minutes from now, with the mark of her palm still red on his jaw, because he'd overheard a rumor on the other side of the room that he thought she should know, so that her business didn't suffer.

Well, maybe not text, since they'd learned their lesson about subpoenaed records, but he'd get the information to her somehow.

"See? What's the worst thing that could happen, if I got drunk and horny?" Mack challenged. "Beyond me getting to hear you say *horny*, which, to be honest, sounds way more vulgar than *fuck you*. I *love* the way you say *fuck you*."

Anne formed her lips around a very sincere F, and then caught herself, her eyes narrowing. He was watching that F-shape of her lips with every appearance of eagerness, and she'd be damned if she'd give him the satisfaction.

"Oh, come *on*," he begged. "Go for it. Now you're just taunting me."

"Mack," she said between her teeth. "If you think I'm wasting my energy on a slap, you don't know me very well. I'm going to knee you right in the groin."

His teeth showed sharp. "Yeah? You going to take it into the physical? Go for it, Anne."

He looked so damn *hungry*. Nerve endings were shooting alive *everywhere*, and they made her almost frantic with the need to do something. Anything. Knee him in the groin.

"Mack Corey, you have lost your mind due to some empty-nest syndrome, and I'm going to restrain myself in consideration. Also, because think of the pictures in the paper tomorrow when I knock you out in your own home. I'd probably get arrested again."

"Why? *I* wouldn't press charges. It would be pretty fucking funny, if you ask me. Especially if you managed to get cake smashed all over yourself in the process. If you want to start a brawl with me, trust me, I'm game."

Her teeth snapped together on the nearly overwhelming urge to smash her head against his to

31

knock some kind of sense into him. "Go dump your head in a bucket of water. Come back when you're using your brain again."

"Already dumped something much more sensitive with a glass of ice water," he said matter-of-factly.

She gaped at him.

"Might have to do it again," he added, with the tiniest flick of his blue gaze down over her body. Hers flicked down his own body involuntarily to—was he aroused *again?*

"Mack." She drew her stomach muscles in tight and pressed her thighs together, against this squirmy *something* that needed to behave.

"I don't know if I've told you this in the past twenty years, but since you're already at the point you're ready to knee me in the groin, I might as well go for it. You're hot, Anne."

She stared at him, her jaw dropped. And *nothing* got her to drop her jaw. Not even an announcement of "Guilty" and "six months in prison".

"I really like that new cut on you." Without dropping the cage of his arms, he nodded to the short, short haircut she had adopted in a moment of temper during her prison sentence.

One of the other women there had plans to open her own hair salon once she got out and kept eyeing Anne's classic bob avariciously, and at a certain point, Anne had just said, *Go for it.* It was a minimum security prison, but they'd still had to get permission to set up the hair salon under strict guards, because of the scissors. Anne was occasionally tempted to disillusion people of their Club Fed illusions about life in a minimum security prison, but she wouldn't give anyone in the media the satisfaction of telling them how horrible it had been.

"Makes you look like some elf queen, all frost and timeless power." Mack gave one of his tight, aggressive grins. "I especially liked the way you told the journalists

32

it was because of prison lice, all while looking like the graceful elf queen. That was pretty damn hilarious."

"I kind of lost patience with idiots, in prison," she admitted. Not that she had ever had too much, but she never used to say things like that. Some shift had occurred, some perversity, some desire to provoke when once she would have held it all in, under calm, cool control.

Telling the journalists she'd had lice had kind of been another way of saying *fuck you.*

"And you're being an idiot right now," she warned him.

He held her eyes with those vivid blue ones of his. The man had never been able to back down from anything or anyone but his own children. Neither had she. "Well, go ahead then, Anne. Lose your patience with me. I dare you."

"I'm mentally counting the glasses of champagne you must have had. To encourage myself to stay tolerant."

"It's sexy as hell," he mentioned. And lifted one hand from the wall to *run his finger down the nape of her neck.* A frisson ran through her. "That haircut. All elegant and cool and remote, and your nape so exposed like that. You have a beautiful neck."

She couldn't stop shivering. It was the strangest thing. As if that one involuntary and perfectly natural shiver that had come from a finger brushing such a sensitive spot just *kept going.* Shivering and shivering through her, this tiny subtle earthquake whose aftershocks were bringing down defenses she'd been taking for granted for decades. Defenses older even than their friendship.

"You're going to be so embarrassed in the morning," she told him desperately. The desperation pissed her off. If she didn't let an idiot grand jury make her desperate, she didn't see why she should give the power to him.

He snorted. "Can't remember the last time I was embarrassed. No, I take that back. When my own daughter was getting headlined as a chocolate thief, that was pretty bad. She finally managed to beat out Jaime's headlines for G8 protests with that one. If I can handle that, I sure as hell can handle the embarrassment of knowing I hit on a woman who froze me out. Especially when she has that little V of pale hair pointing right down to her nape that way." He followed it with his finger again, and again the touch shivered everywhere. "How is a man supposed to keep himself from touching that?"

"I've had this haircut for several months," she said dryly.

"We've been friends for a long time, Anne. I'm used to respecting those walls of yours. But you did agree to be my date for this damn thing, you know."

"I was doing you a favor!" The underhanded—

"I even brought you flowers," he added smugly.

He had, too. Of course, he always brought her flowers when she agreed to go with him to a function. They'd been doing that kind of thing for at least a decade now. It had started, what, a couple of years after the walks on the beach? He'd just asked her, out of the blue, while they were strolling past a beautiful piece of driftwood, to help him out by being his companion at some charity dinner, and what was she supposed to do? Leave him hanging alone?

"Mack Corey. If you want to find yourself fending off money-grubbing, twenty-year-old, wannabe kept women at every single dinner you go to for the rest of your life, just keep this up."

He winced. "Jesus, Anne. That's nasty. All you have to do is raise your eyebrow to wither them, and you're going to abandon me? Cade's based in Paris now!"

Cade had a pretty effective way of raising her eyebrow at younger women who wanted to date her father, too.

"You're bluffing," Mack decided firmly.

Anne raised an eyebrow at him. Nobody knew when she was bluffing, not even Mack. You didn't create a billion dollar empire from scratch by being an easy read.

He didn't noticeably wither at her raised eyebrow, however.

"The thing is, Anne, I'm pretty sure after three dates, a man's supposed to be able to at least get a kiss. And I've lost track of how many dates we've been on. I'd have to lock you up against your doorway when I got you home and kiss you all night before I'd even start to make a dint in the ones you owe."

A sudden and dissolving image of herself locked up just like this between his body and a door, only they were all alone on her porch, sheltered by the climbing roses, with no one to see or stop them but...them. And Mack talked as if he had no intention of stopping.

So...that left it all on her.

"You know what I thought about two seconds after I dashed a glass of ice water over my dick?"

"'Ouch'?" She could not believe Mack Corey was using the word dick in front of her. He did believe in calling a spade a spade, but that didn't usually extend to calling a penis a dick. He'd had to watch his mouth raising two daughters. Although Cade had once confided that her father had personally taught her to say, *Fuck you.* He'd said she would need to be able to at least say it in her head, to survive at the head of a multinational corporation.

He grinned. "After that. I thought, to be precise, *Fuck, God damn it, that's cold.* And then I thought if there was ever in this world a woman who could take anything I threw at her, it would be you, Anne Winters. So why the hell have I spent so much time enjoying those fantasies of you only in the privacy of my own room? It's almost selfish, when you think about it."

She stared at him. Her whole world whirled, and all that whirling seemed to concentrate itself in her erogenous zones. Little spirals, twirling, twirling,

twirling, pressing against her nipples, stirring in her sex, and yes, twisting over the nape of her neck. Fantasies of her? That he'd been enjoying in the privacy of his own room? "What fantasies?" she asked icily.

He grinned. "Oh, good. You want to know."

"Oh, no, I damn well do not, Mack Corey." She ducked under his arm, while her breasts and her sex beat the lie at her, and started to walk away.

A hand caught her arm and swung her right back. She stared at it and then up at him with an incredulity somewhat akin to if he had reached out and drawn a finger down one of the wedding cakes right in front of her and then licked the icing off. "Told you that you'd run," he said, with that glittering challenge in his eyes. "Of course, the problem with running is that then somebody can catch you."

"I want you to go sleep this off, and then we'll talk again tomorrow morning," she said between her teeth.

"Can't. It's our dance." He pulled her toward the floor.

"What do you mean it's our—"

"I danced with Jaime. I danced with Cade. Now I get to dance with my date. Before Dad grabs you."

Anne almost smiled at that. It was true that Jack Corey usually insisted she dance at least once with him. He liked to dance, and he had a healthy fear of twenty-year-olds, too. *It's creepy,* he complained. *They're like vampires. Going for the old rich guy because they're hoping I'll die fast.*

Then he would wink at her. *Now, the last I read, the rule of thumb for a man was he could date anyone half his age plus seven years, so that makes you and me perfect, right? Honestly, you're too old for me.*

Jack Corey was a handful.

"Fine," Anne said, but only because Mack was a fantastic dancer. As soon as she rested one hand on his shoulder, one hand in his, her whole body relaxed, ready to glide around this floor in perfect harmony of movement for hours. "But if you talk anymore, don't sue me for damages later."

"Not a peep." He gave her a cat-got-the-canary smile. "I'll just think."

She stared at him. And then drew a deep breath for patience, and also in the determined hope to breathe all those thoughts he'd stirred up out of her own body and just release them into the atmosphere. Leaving her calm, clear, clean. Like a sea breeze had swept through her and restored her peace.

His hand pressed firm on the small of her back and guided her in close for a turn to get them started. She smiled up at him automatically, because dancing with him *always* made her smile, and then she remembered that she wasn't in a smiling mood. In fact, she was very close to dumping one of his son-in-law's friends' chocolate structures on his head, which would have the added benefit of removing a disruption to her wedding cake arrangements. Possibly erase some of that smug "I am the most perfectionistic genius in the world" arrogance off their faces, too. *No, I am, kids.*

True to his word, Mack didn't speak. He just watched her with a little smile on his face and intent blue eyes and—danced. Danced with power and control and confidence, with grace and strength.

But...here was the thing about Mack. He was the most powerful man in the place, easily. And he knew it. He knew how to dance, and he knew how to control her. But if she wanted to do something—a spin or a dip or just shift the direction of their dancing to another part of the floor so she could catch the caterer's attention—she could just give the tiniest little signal with a pressure of her hand or a subtle leaning of her body, and he would do it. He teased her about her need to lead, but what really happened was that, without losing his control of the dance, he acknowledged her control, too. And it never seemed to lessen his confidence in himself at all.

That confidence, right now, radiated through every pore of his body and into hers. *I know how to handle you.*

Heat spread from his hand, and she couldn't get it to stop. It just poured out of him, into her.

She was used to his hand radiating heat, of course, it was one of the things she loved about dancing with him. Loved the firmness of the heat from his hand, the elusive, all-embracing brush of warmth from his whole body moving in such close harmony with hers. But she normally gathered that heat into her belly and held it there. Let it ride snug at the base of her spine. Right now that heat was misbehaving. Slipping out from where his hand rode like an impudent wildfire, snaking arms down toward her thighs and lingering on the way, stretching up toward her breasts. He pulled her in closer for a turn, and their bodies rubbed just before he dipped her, bringing all her weight into dependence of his hard arm. Into this position of utter trust. *Of course he won't let me fall.* Her body never even stiffened against the dip, never tried to resist it and stay upright at all.

She *loved* that dip. More even than the spin of their bodies close together, or when he twirled her out and brought her in a lovely whirl back in tight against him again. More even than the heat of his hand, or the utter sense of relaxation and aliveness from the perfect way their rhythms matched. She always wanted that dip. That moment, when she was suspended on the weight of his arm wrapped around her, holding her in close to his body while he looked down at her.

She loved that dip so much, she who could not stand to trust anyone, depend on anyone. And she had never, ever let herself wonder why.

"How much *have* you had to drink?" she asked, mostly to throw something challenging into the moment, to throw up walls. But also—how could he be drunk enough to say some of the things he had just said and still dance so well?

Mack brought their joined hands to his mouth, so that for one shocked instant her hand thought he really had caught that French hand-kissing infection from his sons-in-law, their curious, easy public intimacy and sweetness. And possessiveness, of course. *My hand. She belongs to me.* Anne had never belonged to anyone that way. Not like something precious the other person wanted to keep.

But instead of a hand kiss, Mack extended his strong index finger from their clasp and laid it over his lips. *Shh.* He drew the tip of his finger over his firmly closed lips, as if sealing them together, and smiled at her. That little, amused, *smug* damn smile he had when he was beating his opponents.

And her knuckles, the back of her hand, brushed elusively against his jaw and the edge of his mouth, but never really touched his lips at all.

He lowered their hands. But not his gaze. Those blue eyes just *held* hers. Watched her as he turned them, as he danced them around the floor, neatly negotiating the other couples without ever brushing against them and without ever looking away from her.

I promised not to talk. But I'm thinking.

Anne was the one who had to look away. And she *hated* being the one to look away, the one to lower her gaze from a challenge. She pretended she was checking to make sure the wedding guests were all being taken care of.

But he kept *thinking.* It was probably why his hand was so aggressively *hot* like that, reaching into all these places his hand wasn't supposed to go. She could feel his thoughts just *pushing* down between her legs, cupping her breasts, invading her panties, doing things his thoughts should *never* have the nerve to do. His thigh pressed against hers a moment on the next turn, and now his damn pushy thoughts were thrusting a thigh up between her legs, pulling her in to ride on it, *spreading* her legs for him.

She wanted to slap him, or better yet hit him, knee him as she'd threatened, fight him to protect herself from the invasion without her permission, and yet he hadn't said one damn word. He hadn't made one inappropriate touch. He hadn't even flicked that intense blue gaze of his down over her breasts in a lewd way.

For all she really knew, his thoughts could be analyzing the latest stock reports by now, and everything else was in her own head.

She tried thinking about the latest stock reports, too. Numbers blurred in her brain, columns dissolving in a wash of black and white, and she gasped with the sense of vertigo that left in her.

Maybe she needed to buy a new house, make it an even two dozen. Or redecorate one of the ones she had. She grasped onto that, calming, and ideas flooded her brain instantly, driving out his persistent *thinking*. Yes. Maybe she would do something very small. That would be different. Take on that "reduce" movement and show how small spaces could be made workable. Something quiet and private, in some gentle, intimate landscape, low, old mountains, maybe. Maybe she would have the house built from repurposed material. Five hundred square feet, no more; she needed to show she could handle the space challenge better than anyone else.

She'd need to use her outdoor area well, with a space that size. A porch or a patio, a swing for two, canvas loungers. And inside, something delicate to separate the bed from the living area, without reducing the sense of space. It would be a white bed, a queen or a double, maybe, big enough for two people who were comfortable with each other. This fragile white fabric, more a suggestion of fabric than anything else, would drape from a centerpiece above it, like old mosquito netting maybe, and the couple could just reach out and brush fingers across it to release it, let it float down and turn the bed into their little room for two.

The sheets would be old Egyptian cotton, washed so many times there was nothing left in them but softness and comfort, and the two people would stretch out on those sheets and—

Her body flowed into a dip, a hand firm under her waist, her body tucked in safe against hardness, blue eyes holding hers.

Lowering her at just the angle she might be lowered onto a bed.

Sure and strong that arm, suspending her just on the edge of something, her position so entirely precarious and entirely safe. She stared up at him, her heart beating hard.

The song had ended. He straightened her effortlessly, and she took a breath to step back, to say thank you, to mention she needed to check on the caterer, as notes to a new song started.

That firm, strong hand tucked her right back up against him. He set her hand onto his other shoulder. And then he wrapped that arm around her, too, snuggling her in close. His freed hand came to rest on her nape.

Big hand, covering all of it, pulling her head close to his chest. It was like being in a spa. Between the warm firm hand on her nape and the warm firm hand on her lower back, her whole spine wanted to dissolve. Just...sink into him. Let him carry her. Just be weight against weight, body against body.

Think about that bed. That quiet, private bed in the little space for two with those sheets that had been slept on so many times...

His hand rubbed over her nape, gentle but firm. *Here you are. I've got you.*

Her neck unstiffened before she could think, her head sinking against his chest. It was a slow dance, one of the love songs Jaime and Dom had chosen. Couples shifted around them on the dance floor, some leaving before they could be forced into too much intimacy, but more filling the floor, all those couples who said, *Even we can dance a slow dance.* Wives tugging on husbands' hands. *Dance with me.*

God, this was nice.

Terrifying how nice it was. She didn't *do* this. Trust in another person to hold her, keep her.

And it was...sexy. That rubbing of bodies, that strength and heat of his, friction, friction, friction, slow and steady and heating her more and more. Until her breasts hurt and her sex felt clutching and greedy and soft, and her nape, where he kept that gentle, rubbing hold of it, just sent shivers over and over down her spine. Little, resistance-destroying vibrations that spread out through her body.

Oh, hell. Maybe she should just *go* with it. As Mack said, what did they have to lose?

Nothing. Right at that moment, it didn't seem possible that they could ever lose anything. Certainly not twenty years of friendship. Not because of something as hot and sweet as this.

Her lips softened apart, and her head actually started, just started, to turn into his chest so she could kiss it when she realized and took a breath, trying to control herself. But her lips felt funny. As if this static electricity had built up in them from all the rubbing and not been allowed that touch to release.

She curled her lips in so that she could lick them, subtly, without ever showing she had.

Mack's other hand rubbed firm and gentle lower down her spine and—*cupped her ass.*

She started.

He squeezed. Shh. Let your ass do what I tell it to.

And damned if she didn't want to *do* it. Let him handle her ass however he liked.

Her butt even felt all tight and flexing and eager, as if she might like some of those things he liked, too.

Cade and Sylvain whirled by, at what seemed a pretty fast pace for a slow dance, heading in the direction Anne had last seen Jaime and Dom. Sylvain was laughing at his wife, but as they passed, those chocolate eyes of his met Anne's, and he winked at her.

Oh, brother.

"Mack," she hissed.

Mack made a mildly impatient, amused sound and she realized he was looking over her shoulder. He tried not to let her turn, but she managed to twist enough and spotted Cade elbowing Jaime. Jaime looked immediately toward her father, and then her eyes widened to match Cade's. Anne couldn't quite figure out their expressions, and maybe they couldn't figure out what they wanted to feel, either. Astonishment? Glee? Amusement? Confusion? None of the expressions seemed very negative, although Anne found several facets of them aggravating. What was amusing or confusing, exactly? Sylvain just raised a puzzled eyebrow at his wife, when she said something to him, and shrugged one easy shoulder.

Like there was nothing at all unusual in his world at a fifty-three-year-old woman getting her ass grabbed by a man in the middle of the dance floor.

There might be something to be said for the French.

"Sorry," Mack said to her. "How did you manage to raise a so much better-mannered child?"

That made Anne scan the garden for Kurt, of course. He was standing stock still over there by the cakes, staring at them, or more particularly at Mack's hand on her butt, both his eyebrows up. Granted, his expression was a lot harder to read, but probably because his reactions were even more complex than Mack's daughters.

And what business was it of any of theirs anyway? Last she'd looked, *they* were getting on with their lives in the ways they chose.

She shrugged, that close to telling Mack, *Go for it,* that she had to bite her teeth closed in astonishment on the G. She was *not* supposed to be giving Mack any go-ahead signs for this madness.

She hadn't drunk anything more than a glass, after all. She was supposed to be keeping their heads for them.

"How long does this song last exactly?" Because she was starting to *feel* drunk. All soft and...smooshy. Holdable, squeezable. And she didn't do those things. She just didn't.

Ever.

Do those things.

"If the band is smart about where their biggest tip is likely to come from, a long time," Mack said.

And indeed, the band drew out a long crooning of "loooove" and cycled around again.

"Haven't they already sung that verse?"

Mack shrugged. "Apparently, they're smart."

"Is that band helping you sexually harass me?"

He snorted. "I'd have to have power over you to do that, Anne. You know what? Maybe we should go back to me just thinking, not talking. Talking seems to give you something to fight."

She should probably twist free and walk off.

But she didn't.

Because she felt too soft and smooshy and holdable. And what if her bones didn't work? What if they just folded up under her the second she tried to stand without support, all floppy, the way they felt?

Also, how thin was her skirt? Was it at all possible a damp spot could show through if this rubbing kept up? She'd never, ever had to worry about that kind of question before.

"Maybe I should dump the ice in one of those champagne buckets on your head. *Or whatever part of your anatomy needs it.*" Again.

"Shhhh," Mack whispered, long and low, so that the sound just shivered everywhere. He pressed *her* finger to his mouth this time. "I'm thinking." And he *bit* it, a firm, tiny pinch of teeth.

Fire raced through her, an unfamiliar burning she had no idea how to put out. "Malcolm Anthony Corey, you are messing with the wrong person." *Yes, dare him. Dare him.* She knew exactly how Mack Corey responded to dares. To being told he couldn't do something.

"Anne. Shut up and dance."

Chapter 4

A nne peeked through the roses, not really spying, no, just...checking up on things. Making sure everything was all right.

Rich, sweet, lemony scent surrounded her. She'd planted the beautiful, pink climber rose with her own hands, to replace a dying one that Julie had planted. It and many of the other roses in her gardens and the Corey ones were in the middle of their spectacular second burst of blooms for September. Anne had helped Julie design these gardens long ago, and given that Mack didn't pay much attention to house and garden design, had had to keep tinkering with and maintaining them ever since. First because somebody had to step in and help the family get through those initial years without Julie and then just because...well, that was what she did. Design spaces. Make the world perfect.

And she'd had time, because somehow, the periods she spent at this house compared to any of the others kept stretching, and so did Mack's. Especially after the girls went away to college, and his house in Corey grew so empty, Mack came here more and more, and somehow they just always stretched their stays at the same time, shifting many aspects of their operations here so they could linger longer. It was when Mack wasn't there, though, that Anne usually came over and worked on his gardens. She didn't know why, but when she didn't have those beach walks with him, something about working in his gardens instead of her own eased her skin.

The Corey beach house had a nice, large, dramatic layout to work with: that line of great French doors that opened the whole house to the sea and sun when the weather was right, and that were filled with glowing, golden promise when you came toward them from the sea at night; the garden that was not too grandiose but that lent itself to a landscape of cozy spots and adventurous, fairytale corners for the girls, and even an old, shared platform for pirate adventures that had a ladder reaching up to it from both yards.

Cade stood under it now, a hand on the ladder as if she was half thinking about climbing up into it despite her sea-green, matron-of-honor finery and high heels, but she turned back to Sylvain instead. He bent his black head to her and lifted his hand to her face, and Anne's mouth softened a little, this strange mix of happiness and wistfulness, as she watched them. She would have liked to have a daughter. Maybe, somewhere, she would have liked to have a man like Sylvain Marquis lifting a tender hand to her cheek.

"Happy?" Sylvain asked his wife, in that low, warm voice of his that made Anne think of chocolate with a French accent. One of Paris's top chocolatiers—*the* top chocolatier, he preferred to claim—he had a gorgeous poet look going on that made him a media darling. She needed to get him on her show. She'd bet he would make a nice boost to her post-prison-comeback ratings. Her viewers would go wild.

Cade nodded, that smile on her face caught by the moonlight and the lights Anne had had woven through the garden. Her light brown hair had been coerced into an elegant updo for her role as matron of honor, including elegant strands twining gently down by her face. Sylvain clearly didn't like it—his long, pianist's fingers would start to touch the sculpted hair, hover, then curl back toward his palms and find another target. Her cheekbone, her eyebrow, a rub over the join of her neck and shoulder that made Cade's shoulder and neck flex a little in pleasure.

Anne suspected that Sylvain's reluctance to touch her hairdo was less out of respect for its elegance than because only a heavy coating of hairspray had gotten Cade's silky fine, straight hair to stay up. Cade's first ballet recital after her mother's death, Anne had been the one to take over Julie's role and glue Cade's hair to her head to last the performance. Well, someone had to fly into Corey and help out in the wake of that car wreck. The family had fallen to pieces. Anne knew how to pick up pieces.

Carefully. Trying not to get anyone cut on them.

Someone always did get cut, though. Cade, in the middle of Anne's careful work on her hair, had suddenly bowed her head into her hands and started crying. But she'd had a lead role in the performance, and she'd forced herself on anyway, that way she did. She'd started crying onstage again, in the middle of one of her solos, tears running down her cheeks as she danced determinedly through. Probably Mack, as griefstruck and lost as his girls, had encouraged her to go on, convinced it would be good for her to pursue the ballet like normal, and his encouragement had operated on Cade with the usual force expectations had on her: she always wanted to fulfill them, surpass them. So she'd felt it was her *duty* to do this next ballet performance, rather than just something her father was hoping would help get her through the grief. It had been, in the end, a bit too much for a thirteen-year-old used to having her mother there beaming at her for every performance.

"I can't believe my dad," Cade said now.

Anne winced and started to step back.

Sylvain laughed. "What? Your *belle-mère* is hot. Or not your mother-in-law, but whatever you call her."

Anne's eyebrows shot up. Sexy poet-chocolatier, media darling, and expert flirt Sylvain Marquis thought she was hot? He was younger than her own son!

Also, he thought she was in some way in the role of a mother-in-law?

"Hey," Cade protested, but she was smiling, secure and unthreatened. "You're married."

"Caught," Sylvain agreed with great mournfulness, pulling his wife more snugly into his arms and rocking her against him. "My days of flirting with hot, elegant older women are over."

"Not so they'd notice," Cade said dryly.

Anne bit back a laugh. It was true. Sylvain didn't think he was flirting? What did he do to women when he ramped it up?

Sylvain leaned back against one of the tables and pulled Cade between his legs. "Are you serious that your dad has known her twenty years? And this is the first time he's hit on her? Do you think I should give him *tips* or something?"

Cade started to chortle. Anne almost did, too. Her nostrils stung with the effort to hold back this eruption of, of *giggles* at the thought of the expression on Mack's face as Sylvain Marquis gave him lessons in flirting.

"They're *friends*, Sylvain."

Sylvain gave her a look as if she'd been dropped on her head. "*Pardon,* but if I'd been fantasizing about a friend that hot for twenty years, I'd have done something about it long before this."

"Sylvain. My mother was still alive twenty years ago."

Sylvain squeezed his wife's shoulder in apology, reconsidered, and waved one hand. "*Enfin,* at some point in the past ten years, at least."

"Do you really think he's been fantasizing about her for at least ten years?"

"Has she looked that hot for the past ten years?"

You know, Anne had always liked the French. She'd been having a few doubts about that affection ever since she had to actually deal with a horde of them in her kitchens, but maybe her original instincts had been right. *Great* culture.

"Sylvain! She's—that's just rude, to even think of her that way."

Sylvain's eyebrows went up. "*Sérieusement? Merde,* I'm never going to understand what counts as good manners in your country."

"It's just that she's so elegant."

"I *know*," Sylvain said in exaggerated hungry, yummy tones.

Cade gave him a pretend hit on the shoulder. "And she's so cool, and, and walled-off."

"*Exactly*. How has your dad managed to hold off his attack for so long?"

Anne's whole body was starting to tickle. She'd been hit on by younger men a *lot*. She had an exceptional degree of money and power, and there were plenty of men who found both those things attractive. Especially if they thought they could sleep their way to having that money and power for themselves. But Sylvain didn't want her money and power. He didn't even care about that kind of thing. If you even suggested it, he'd raise those supple eyebrows and go into fits of Gallicness: *Moi? Sylvain Marquis? Moi?* All black-haired, brown-eyed arrogance and passion.

He didn't even want *her*, in fact. He was very happily married. And somehow that all combined together so that this casual discussion of her *hotness*, by someone that young and sexy himself, while the imprint of a hand still tingled against her butt, made her—

Tickle. Curled her toes. Left her whole body restless.

"What?" Sylvain's laughing voice, all of him focused on teasing Cade. "When you did that to me, it was all I could think about, how to bring those walls down."

Anne backed away. And that was not at all because she was fleeing this conversation. She didn't flee. But she *did* exercise good manners and object to eavesdropping. Eventually. At least when that eavesdropping got uncomfortable.

Sylvain's voice caught her one last time as she slipped away. "I'll bet you a new Cade Marquis line of chocolate bars that it's all he can think about, too."

***

"Took you long enough," Jack Corey said gleefully from the lush greenery that turned their heated pool into a tropical oasis, popping out right in the middle of Mack's hunt for a certain fleeing prey.

Oh, good God. Mack held up a hand. "Dad. Don't even start." They were too near the deep end of that pool. Mack might end up pushing him in.

But of course his father's eyes just gleamed with more delight, bluer than the chlorine-free water. Everyone swore Mack had inherited Jack's blue eyes. "I was beginning to think you were scared."

Mack's teeth snapped together instantly. "I was— what?"

"*I* was going to start going after her myself. Letting a woman like that go to waste for so long. I don't know where I went wrong raising you." Jack Corey shook his white head mournfully. "I *tried* to teach you to go after what you want."

Damn it, how did his father still manage to make his head explode within seconds in any conversation, after more than fifty damn years? "Good thing I went ahead and taught myself how to really do it." Mack made his voice as patronizing as he could and gave a patting motion to the air for good measure. "Not that there's anything wrong with making a few million, Dad. Don't get me wrong. You did what you could." Implication: *So did I. And guess whose "could" was bigger?*

Jack Corey narrowed his eyes at him. "You're standing on the shoulders of giants, kid."

Well...true. His own father and grandfather. It was why Mack had had to get so damn big himself, in order to beat them.

Well, and because his dad was so damn provoking. Mack in his twenties had wanted nothing more than to say: *Oh, you think your multimillion-dollar US candy company is something? Watch me take over the world with it.*

And he had, hadn't he? Thirty percent of the cacao production in the world, and so many subsidiaries, doing so many things so smoothly, that he had to keep taking over struggling companies to restructure into something successful just to keep life interesting. The more struggling the better, really. *Nobody else can make this work? Watch me.*

And his girls didn't want any of it.

Acted as if it was some kind of goddamn *bad* thing he'd done, sometimes, capturing the world for them and laying it at their feet.

So it was easier to focus on his aggravating father. Besides, if Jack Corey could say outrageously unfounded things to provoke him, Mack didn't know why he should have to play nicer. "You gave me a decent handful of change to get started."

His father's mouth opened and closed, most satisfyingly like a fish. "A decent amount of change!"

Mack shrugged. "Gave me something to work with." You could play around with a few million, not to mention you grew up learning the business ropes and forming the initial contacts, understanding the industry and the stock market and knowing what the people who controlled it looked like when they had a bad cold, just like any other person. Anne, starting from her family of middle-class professors, had only managed to get up to a billion so far. Of course, that was also partly because there was only so far an empress could extend her empire without delegating, something Anne had a hard time doing, but still. He bit back a grin. *Only managed a billion.* He'd have to put it to her that way sometime when he wanted to get her riled up.

Shit, *yeah*, the erotic charge that went through him at the idea of getting Anne riled up.

"You're trying to change the subject from your own inadequacies," Jack Corey said severely, waving a hand.

From his—Mack took a deep breath that just kind of sizzled through his teeth when he let it out. "Dad. You're pushing it."

"With women," his father argued, *as if he was perfectly justified*, one of his father's most infuriating paternal traits.

"Dad. I'm warning you."

"Well. How long have you been mooning over her?"

Mooning? "Dad. She's my friend! Quit being so damn...sexist." What the hell had he just said? His father made his brain short-circuit. He was the only person in the whole damn world who could do that to Mack's brain. Well, Anne, once in a while, but that was usually because his brain had taken a sudden trip south in the middle of a conversation and he was busy trying to hide it.

Jack chortled, entirely delighted at the opening. "It's not sexist to want a hot woman. It's human."

"Dad. I thought we agreed that I got enough of your advice about sex when I was twelve."

His father gave him a superior look out of a face so deeply wrinkled it was an alarming foreshadowing of what Mack was going to look like if his blood pressure let him survive another thirty years. "Clearly you need more."

"Oh, good God." Mack tried to turn away. Mostly because he was pretty sure if he pushed his father into the pool, Jack Corey would manage to grab his ankle or something and drag him in, too. And wouldn't *that* photo end up circulating on his daughters' TV screens forever. He'd go down in legend to their great-grandchildren. Not the guy who had made them multiple billions as a legacy, but the man who pushed his own father into a pool at a wedding. He'd probably be the bad guy in the story, too. *Nobody* would remember how provoking Jack Corey was.

"Anyway, last I checked, squeezing a woman's ass was still considered sexist," Jack Corey said regretfully.

"I don't know how that happened. You could get away with that kind of thing when I was your age."

"No, you could not, Dad. Maybe when you were twenty, but you're probably fantasizing the past again." Mack re-adopted his patronizing, pat-him-on-the-head tone. "I hear old guys tend to do that."

Jack Corey grinned. *Touché*. It was always hard to fight with his dad, because his dad tended to *like* it when his son scored one off him. "So what took you so long to make a move on her?" The elder Corey's fighting spirit had relaxed with his grin, and now it was a genuine question. *We got our sparring out of the way. Now let's talk about what matters.*

For all the old man drove him crazy...damn, but he had a good dad.

Mack hesitated a long moment, his hands in his trouser pockets under his tux jacket. Exactly the way he always stuck his hands in his jeans pockets when he walked on the beach with Anne. So he didn't reach for something he shouldn't. His own voice went quiet, like it did sometimes at the oddest moments with his dad. As if he was still a kid, still glad to have a father for counsel. "Dad. I've never in my life had a friend as good as she is. I'll never have another one. If she doesn't want it, then I'm not going to do it."

Jack Corey gave that some thought. "But you still did something. There on the dance floor."

"I know. I just—I can't—that prison. It still makes me want to rip everything. Rip up the whole world." *And I hugged her. And God damn but does she feel good, nestled up against my damn dick like that. Now I can't separate the reality anymore from all those years of fantasy. I don't want to. I want to rip that damn sheet of plastic between us all away.* "She stands over there at the edge of things, like none of this has even touched her, like we're still the same people we were before her trial started, and it makes me want to get to her."

Jack Corey nodded and considered another long moment. Suddenly he grinned again and shook his head. "You're a funny kid."

"What?" Was he ever going to get through a conversation with his father without pounding his head against a wall? And yet—it was kind of disorientingly reassuring to still have one person alive in the world who was capable of seeing him as a funny kid.

"Well, you say she's your best friend. You've known each other twenty years. And you still don't realize that if you try to get to Anne Winters and she doesn't want you to, she'll stop you?"

Chapter 5

O h, good God. There was happiness all over this place. Anne stopped again in the shadow of a tree, smiling a little. Still pretending to herself that she wasn't doing this on purpose, spying on the people under her wing, but she really was. Slipping from place to place in the gardens she had designed to be a refuge for group laughter and intimate moments both, reassuring herself from the confusion of Mack's behavior with sighting after sighting of contentment. *I made the space for them to have that.*

The lighting she had designed for the wedding played beautifully over Jaime and Dom, soft and sheltering, a gentle cocoon of mellow gold against the darkness. The sound of the sea shushed steadily over the dunes, and the little waterfall in this nook trickled in sweet counterpoint.

Jaime brought her hands up over her head and twirled with joy, spinning away from her big, rough-looking new husband as if there was too much of that happiness to stand still for it, whirling back to land with a rush against his chest as if she had to hurry back to that joy's source. Dom caught her. Anne was pretty sure that man would always catch her.

And it gave her a solid feeling in her stomach, a belief that maybe some joys in this world, some couples, could make it through.

Jaime danced a little against Dom as she clasped her hands behind his neck, and he cooperated, rocking them gently as if they could still hear the last love song in their heads.

Jaime snuggled against his chest, and Anne was considering her possible avenues for retreat without disturbing them, when Jaime laughed, in almost sleepy contentment. "Did you see my dad? Do you think he's drunk?"

Dom grunted, this remnant of an irascibility that too much happiness had almost drugged to sleep. Dom dealt poorly with Mack. Didn't trust a man that powerful so close to him or to Jaime, Anne was pretty sure. Mack did a little better with Dom from his side, mostly because, as he had explained to Anne one morning on the beach, whatever Dom's faults, *and there are many* Mack's gravel morning voice had added, he was pretty sure the man would do anything for Jaime.

"I thought you told me those two were already together," Dom said.

Anne's eyebrows went up.

"Well, they're discreet about it," Jaime said. "I guess they didn't want to upset me and Cade when we were teenagers. Or maybe just didn't want to let the world into their business, because the world is pretty damn nosy about us. But I'm pretty sure they've been a lot more than friends for, what, probably a decade now."

What?

"It's sweet," Jaime said. "I think it makes them both so much happier. Although they're both a hard read."

Dom shook that black head of his. He was fresh-shaved and very elegant in a tuxedo for his wedding, although a secret rebel's tuxedo, with an open neck to his white shirt. But he would always have this sexy, big, dangerous thing going on.

Well, what? Anne's mouth curved in her shadows. If her sons-in-law—if *Mack's* sons-in-law—were going around thinking she was hot, she had the right to admit to herself they were pretty hot, too, didn't she?

"I don't know what they might have had when you were a teenager, but if they did have something going on, he screwed up or something happened, and she cut him off," Dom said definitely. "And he's been cut off for a while. Your dad looks at her like she's a castle he's about to bring down."

Oh, he did, did he? All Anne's forces manned her walls in defensive instinct, just at the thought. She hadn't built those castle walls to be penetrable. She'd built them to withstand a siege.

And somewhere, deeper, lower down, like this secret tunnel that some spy inside her wanted to open to the enemy: *He did, did he? He wanted in that badly?*

Jaime laughed. "Well, she'd better watch out then. Because once my dad starts his pieces across a chessboard, he wins. Even if he has to knock the whole damn table over and go for the other player's throat to do it."

*****

Mack nodded at the guard stationed near the boardwalk coming in over the dunes and walked down it until he came to the bend in it, a couple of benches and a space where people wanting to get closer to the ocean but not quite in the mood to get sand in their feet could sit and watch it. He shrugged his shoulders, glad to escape the noise and wedding hustle for a while, shaking his dad's aggravation off him but letting the thoughts from it sink in.

The moon and starlight shone bright on the water. He made way for a shadowy couple coming up the ramp from the beach, a couple that resolved itself into Summer and Luc. The moonlight shone off Summer's golden hair, her hand in Luc's as Luc angled them a little so that she could precede him up the boardwalk while they still held hands. Summer's luminous gold and Luc's black hair and black eyes made it look as if light was being trailed by shadow up the walk. Summer had Luc's tuxedo jacket over her shoulders, and Luc's white shirt was open several buttons at the neck. The wind or maybe fingers had ruffled his hair.

Summer had that gentle half-smile on her face that made Mack kind of mentally snap a picture of it and send it to Julie. Not that he exactly believed Julie was somewhere getting those mental emails of his, but he didn't exactly not believe it, either. He'd always had that habit of thinking out to her at some moments, like a little nudge through death: *You see Cade giving that valedictorian speech? Shit, you would have been proud. Or, Good God, Julie, tear-gassed at a G8 summit. What the hell am I going to do with that girl? We should never have named her after my father. I told you that was asking for trouble.*

And now, no words, really, just a nudge of Summer's smile toward that memory of Julie. Because Julie had always worried about Summer, when she was still alive, and Mack thought she'd like to see how happy the girl was now. That fake, silky smile thing she had had going on for so long—that smile-for-the-tabloids—had always made him want to just grab her father Sam's head and beat it against something. But this—this was quieter. Easier. A real happiness.

Maybe he could kind of see how that rounded belly and smile could wrench pain right through a woman who didn't have it.

Summer lifted a hand in acknowledgement, her smile changing for her honorary uncle Mack but still a warm smile, still a real one, Mack was proud to say. She sure as hell didn't smile with real warmth for her own dad. Luc nodded briefly at him as they passed. "Monsieur."

Good kid. Arrogant as hell, like Sylvain and Dom, but good manners on him about it. Mack had genuine trouble dealing with men who weren't arrogant, mostly because they just kind of disappeared before him without him even noticing they existed. Kind of like the straw house for the big bad wolf. Worse than that, really. More like the big bad wolf talking a breath in front of a house, only to have it waver out of existence like smoke just from that intake into his lungs. It was nice to run up against someone made of actual brick from time to time.

He thought of Anne, that lofty, beautiful castle made of smooth, impenetrable stone, and grinned, resting his folded arms on the rail. The ocean looked beautiful at night, all dark and quiet but with the moonlight shining off it. Anne hadn't escaped to here, either. He'd find her in a minute. There was only so far Anne could allow herself to retreat—she'd built herself into a castle to hold her ground, not yield it—and anyway, give her two minutes away from the wedding celebration and all the thoughts of what the wedding organizer might be screwing up would start eating her brain alive, if she didn't go make sure.

He turned and leaned back against the rail, gazing at his house. It felt good to be the owner of that house right about now. It felt as if he'd built this great, big shelter and invited warmth and happiness to come in and stay. Laughter and voices came from the terrace and verandas, the open windows, the tables and the dance floor in the middle of the fairytale-lit gardens and the clusters of people all over the place, a mix of Corey-side guests and all those chef frenemies of Dom's. He didn't know whether Jaime had just been trying to pad Dom's side of the church so he wouldn't stand so isolated, or what, but it felt as if she'd invited half the arrogant chefs in France. Since Cade had been up there as the maid— grrr, *matron*, a word Mack couldn't wrap his mind around when it came to his daughter—of honor, Sylvain had sat on Dom's side of the church, too. Sometimes Mack was afraid he might just have to start liking Sylvain.

He tried to keep it close to his chest, though. No sense letting *Sylvain* know. Jesus.

Jaime had basically just packed up one of the family planes with Dom's chef—was frenemies the right word? They weren't enemies who pretended to be friends, they were guys who solidly had each other's back all while pretending to be enemies, and, hell, but Mack would like to have some enemies like that. To those chef-rival-friend-whatevers, she'd added Dom's staff and the surprisingly large number of other people who actually seemed to like that son-of-a-bitch and flown them over for the wedding.

Which meant Mack had a house packed with men who thought they were gods, and it's not that he had a problem with the conviction, but it wasn't like he was running a Greek pantheon here. What the hell would that make him, Zeus?

He smiled a little as the idea sank in, enjoying owning Olympus. There, lounging against the gazebo railing, was Apollo, for example. That blond chef who looked as if he should be out there on the ocean surfing was busy provoking everyone with a lazy grin, his arm always draping over this tiny, black-haired woman's shoulders as if he needed her to support his weight. Sarah? was that her name? had gotten into the kitchen, too, but apparently Anne had been able to stand her, because she was quiet and perfectionist and not overtly bossy. They were talking to a short woman with spiky, punk hair—Célie, Dom's saucy head chef chocolatier. A blonde woman with a high-end professional camera was capturing photos of the group as if she couldn't stop, while an older, dark-haired chocolatier—in his forties, maybe—occasionally reached out and took her by the camera and pulled her into him, smiling down at her and making her come out from behind it.

Standing near them, reacting to some provocation, was that big lion guy who'd caused Anne a fit over the macarons she'd had planned for the reception. Apparently, he'd winced, and then winced, and then winced some more, and then he'd started flinging orders at Anne's staff and pretty soon he and a couple of those other chefs had taken completely over. Several members of the staff had nearly quit in a huff, and from what Anne said, the Macaron Lion had only shrugged: *Good riddance.*

Since inherently perfectionist and impossibly demanding Anne agreed with him, once she saw the difference between Macaron Guy's work and her people's, it had been pretty funny helping Anne vent her way through the episode. Anne clearly wanted to hit nearly everyone involved over the head, and also find a way to hire Macaron Guy to be on her staff. Something

61

that would never work. Alpha personalities who had to dominate all the space around them and make everything go their way did *not* deal well with Anne.

Well, except him. He gave the guys around the gazebo a smug little smile. *Beat you.* Mostly, probably, because he was older and while it had made him less flexible in some ways, it had also taught him not to be such a shit-ass.

You could stand to make yourself a bit supple, to have a woman as strong as Anne in your camp.

He scanned the gardens and veranda and the glass windows that let him see inside the great house, waiting to catch a glimpse of her. Instead, he spotted Jaime out in the gardens over there by the little waterfall. Jaime's red-brown hair was still too short to be put in those braids he'd loved so much when she was a freckle-faced, gap-toothed kid. No, she had this elegant jaw-sweeping thing going on right now that made her look so grown-up. Damn it. But beautiful. He sure as hell had two beautiful daughters.

She was twirling into Dom's arms, laughing up at him. Like she used to dance up to her daddy and laugh up at *him*, goddammit. Glumness settled over Mack again.

Paris.

Why the hell did they have to choose Paris?

He could go to Paris, he supposed. They'd bought that damn sterile penthouse apartment there last year just to make it easier on him and his dad to visit, and to make sure his girls always had a refuge if they needed to get away from those idiot boyfriends of theirs. He could pretty much tell that wouldn't be necessary by now, but back then, what had he known about those arrogant s.o.b.'s?

Looked as if he was stuck with them now. It was a good stuck, he knew it deep down, but...shit. It made his shoulders feel so heavy. As if, for one of the first times in his life, they wanted to sag.

He could set up at least part-time headquarters in Paris, easily enough. Well, easily compared to some of the other things he did running a multibillion-dollar corporation. But if they'd wanted to be on the same side of the ocean as their father, they probably would have said so by now.

He glowered at his toes, feeling empty, empty, like someone had sucked all his air out of him and left him this limp balloon washed up on the beach.

Plus, shit, even if he did move his whole headquarters to Paris—would Anne move hers?

And as he thought that, he thought—well, everything. His lungs filled, and his shoulders straightened, as if he'd just breathed the whole world back into him.

Anne. Anne. Shit. If a man thought about a woman *that* way, that he couldn't even move closer to his daughters without making sure she was going to move with him, then he needed to do something about it.

A little lightning bolt of greedy pleasure lanced through him as he thought about doing something about it.

Maybe his life wasn't halfway over but halfway started. And *fuck* with this platonic shit. *Jesus*, he was getting tired of looking at her ass and not touching it. The *things* he had done to her in his fantasies in the privacy of his shower. She'd probably castrate him if he tried a couple of them in real life, but as to the rest of them...hell. If there was one thing Mack had figured out before he was even out of his teens: nothing ventured, nothing gained.

He'd been eyeing that gorgeous, queen's castle a long time. Trying to make himself hold off, respect their treaties, keep his ally. But that fundamental greed pushed at him, that need to claim every territory he wanted. About high time he ripped those treaties up and laid siege.

Well, siege. He was fifty-three years old and he'd been on the other side of that moat a hell of a long time already. Maybe it was time to bring in some cannons.

Chapter 6

“ Ha. Caught you,” Mack said, stepping up so close his biceps brushed her shoulder. “Hiding in front of the house now? Chicken.”

Chicken? Her? She snapped her teeth together. “Mack Corey, I am watching your first son-in-law and his friends ruin your second son-in-law’s car. Don’t spoil the moment.”

It was kind of a hot moment, to be honest. Since they were going around talking about people’s hotness out loud these days. The chefs had stripped down to their white shirts, or in Patrick’s case the edgier black T-shirt he wore under his tux, and, sleeves rolled up, they were attacking that car with melted chocolate like kids given finger paints. All those intensely physical, creative men, full of energy and passion, letting their inner four-year-old out.

Mack grinned. “It’s Jaime’s old car from college, really. Cade said at their wedding in France that the French didn’t get into this whole car-sabotage tradition.”

“Yes, well, now that someone has explained it to them, they’re taking to it.”

They were, too. The chefs were laughing their heads off as they coated the car in chocolate, drawing elaborate messages and designs as they attempted to one-up each other. The photographers were having a field day. That blonde one who was married to one of the older chocolatiers hadn’t let her camera stop clicking once.

“Well,” Sylvain told Cade with a wink, glancing over and making sure his voice was loud enough for Mack to hear. “You can’t *eat* Corey Chocolate. You might as well do something with it.”

Cade, as deep in the buckets of the melted chocolate as the chefs, promptly smeared a handful of it on Sylvain's face.

"Seriously," Mack growled, "how I stand him..."

Sylvain grabbed Cade and kissed the chocolate onto *her* face.

Mack groaned and tilted his head back to gaze at the sky.

Anne forgot she was avoiding him and patted his arm in pseudo-consolation, struggling not to laugh.

"You call this decoration?" Jack Corey asked, gleefully signing COREY + RICHARD over the bumper. "I expected some of your fancy curlicues at the least."

"To get blown off on the road?" Sylvain asked, with great offense. "*My* chocolate?"

Philippe Lyonnais flicked a big melted blob of the Corey chocolate at him from the other side of the car.

It hit Sylvain square on one of those arrogant eyebrows. Mack gave a delighted grunt. Both Sylvain's eyebrows went up. He turned, grinned—and then the chocolate battle broke out.

"Uh-oh." Anne ducked behind Mack as within seconds nearly every chef around the car was involved. Roars capable of dominating the noisiest kitchens filled the air as great handfuls of melted chocolate flew and spattered.

"Hey!" Mack protested, wincing as a stray spray of chocolate caught him on the face. "You're blocking my ability to maneuver!" Visibly so, as he started to duck instinctively and caught himself so that she didn't take the chocolate instead of him. That blob hit him square in the shoulder, right where her face would have been had he ducked.

She darted out to the shelter of a bush, as Sylvain grinned and started aiming straight for Mack on purpose. Mack grinned like a devil as soon as Anne freed him for movement and launched straight into the volley, going for Sylvain's bucket of melted chocolate.

While the volley went on all around them—even Luc Leroi getting drawn into it, after that blond Patrick went after him until he cracked—Mack and Sylvain rolled on the ground, fighting for the bucket and managing to get themselves thoroughly drenched in its contents.

Anne was laughing so hard her ribs hurt. She couldn't remember laughing that hard in nearly *ever*, before prison. In prison itself, she and some of the other inmates had managed to drive themselves into some surprising bouts of giddy female laughter over the craziest things sometimes. It would be strange if locked up in prison was where she had learned how to release herself.

"Guys! Stop, *stop!*" the wedding organizer called from the steps of the house. "They're coming!"

Nobody listened to her, of course.

If you wanted something done right...Anne sighed and came out from the bush, lifting her arms in a dramatic cut gesture.

The place was a chocolate battlefield. The guys were the worst, but their female partners clearly hadn't been able to resist the temptation, and even the photographer one, clicking away, had caught some in her hair. Laughing, sneaking in final vengeances against their nearest enemies, they slowly subsided in response to Anne's gestures.

She advanced. The battle froze with her every step, as the chefs dropped their hands and took their enemy's last glob of chocolate without vengeance, rather than risk messing *her* up. They diverted their energy into grabbing girlfriend or wife and wrapping her laughing protests up against a chocolate-covered body.

Anne stepped through the mess immaculate, even down to her shoes, until she was standing beside Mack Corey by the car. "I thought we agreed on bubbles and fireworks to escort the bridal couple out," she said very mildly.

Mack, on the ground beside Sylvain, both of them so doused in chocolate they could have been mud-wrestling, yielded the bucket to Sylvain with great reluctance as both men flopped onto their backs and grinned up at her.

There. Peace had been established. Order would be restored. In the entire area around the car, she was the only person without a speck of chocolate on her. No one, of course, dared touch *her*.

Even in prison, she'd had the power to make sure people left her entirely alone. No one tried to reach across her plate, or step into her space, or do any of those other things those internet guides to surviving prison said she wasn't supposed to let them do. Not once she lifted her chin and looked at them.

She gave the wedding organizer one of those little looks now. *Presence, woman. Get some.*

Then she looked back down at Mack, smugly. Queen to muddy peasant at her feet. This was a nice position for them. She let her look tell him that, almost, almost tempted to ruin one of her shoes by nudging him delicately with her toe like some messy captive at her feet, just to emphasize the point.

Mack's gaze ran up and down her once. He shook his chocolate-smeared head. "Anne, sweetheart. That's such a pretty dress, I really hate to do this to you, but—" His hand shot up to lock around her wrist and yank her down on top of him before she could even blink. She landed with a thud and a great smearing of chocolate. Mack grinned. "Not really," he admitted. "Really that was a lot of fun." He smeared a handful all over her hair for good measure.

Almost, almost he got a squeal out of her. A squeal! Anne bit it back just in time so it might have come out, maximum, as the tiniest noise strangled in her throat and pushed herself up from his chest to stare down at him. "You are trying to die young."

He just grinned. "Aww. You and my dad are probably the only people here who think I can still do that."

His grin kicked through her, making her want to grin, too, making that laughter want to just bubble out of her again. And right then the doors opened, the wedding organizer making noises of despair, and Jaime and Dom stepped out.

Anne pushed out of Mack's slippery hold to her feet, while Sylvain and Mack scrambled up, too, reaching hands to help each other in an instinctive and unnoticed gesture of mutual support that made Anne bite back another grin.

Dom stopped stock still, staring at them.

Jaime brought her hands to her mouth, gazing from the decorated car to the utter mess they had made of each other and starting to laugh.

"He started it," Sylvain claimed, pointing at Philippe.

Philippe pressed an innocent, chocolate hand to his chest and pointed a finger right at the next nearest chef, big, roaring Gabriel. Gabriel grinned and pointed at Patrick. Patrick pointed at Luc.

Luc raised his eyebrow at him, but since that eyebrow had chocolate on it, the look was hilarious. Even *Luc* was grinning, all that brilliant passion and emotion he usually packed into a small smile breaking completely free. And, whoa, talk about hot. Anne needed to get Luc Leroi on her show, too. Actually, maybe she needed to go ahead and book all of these guys while she had them in her vicinity. She could fly to Paris and rent a studio there for the shoots.

Patrick changed his accusing finger and pointed it at little, usually serious Sarah. Sarah laughed, and Patrick kissed her when she did, entirely delighted with her and with himself.

Damn, all this easy, happy kissing going on around her made her feel so...lonely. So untouchable. Except...she looked down at her thoroughly chocolate-smeared dress. Was that Mack Corey's chocolate handprint on her arm?

Dom and Jaime made their careful way toward the car, Jaime lifting her skirts high.

"Um...I think maybe we'll come back and hug everyone tomorrow?" Jaime said.

"We're more a kissing kind of culture," Sylvain told her, presenting her with one of his chocolate-streaked cheeks.

Jaime laughed and pulled back into Dom, who wrapped an arm instantly around her. "We'll say it's the thought that counts tonight."

Dom was looking at the decorated car, which had survived surprisingly well, as the chefs were more intent on attacking other people than their work. It was covered with well-wishes and *Just Married* in two languages and even a beautiful caricature of Dom and Jaime and their...seven predicted children, the whole surrounded by dozens of little hearts.

Mack raised a hand high and snapped his fingers.

"Oh, fireworks!" the wedding organizer exclaimed. Seriously, that woman.

But within seconds of the organizer speaking into her tiny headset, the fireworks started going off. Dom looked up at them as the colors burst across the night sky. Then he looked back at the car and all the chefs who had decorated it for him, staring a long moment before he flushed deeply suddenly, shoving his hands across his face. Jaime slipped her arm around his waist to give him a squeeze. That relaxed him, but it was still a visibly choked-up Big Bad Dangerous Rebel who got behind the wheel of the car and drove away.

Sylvain grinned smugly in his wake, a spectacle of diabolical chocolate-ness. "How long before he realizes I drew a line of chocolate all the way around the steering wheel, do you think?"

"I warned you how much trouble you're going to be in if he accidentally gets it all over Jaime's wedding dress and it won't come out, didn't I?" Cade said.

"Look, *I* didn't start this weird American car tradition." Sylvain just grinned some more. "She should have changed. Anyway, think of how she'll explain it to her daughters when she tries to pass the wedding dress on."

Cade laughed.

Anne drew a breath and sighed it out.

Daughters.

How easily people assumed something so magical would happen. How easily they took for granted that if you wanted kids, they would come. She hoped nothing ever shattered their confidence. She hoped—she really did—that all the dreams they took for granted came true. She glanced around for Kai and Kurt, but they hadn't even heard the comment, holding hands, laughing while Kurt wiped a smear of chocolate off Kai's face. They clearly hadn't engaged in battle as intensely as the competitive chefs, who were predisposed to food warfare anyway, but they had certainly gotten into the fun.

Laughing, the chocolate-covered participants all posed agreeably for the pictures the photographers begged—Anne and Mack included—and then people slowly started to dissipate to clean up their sticky selves. Most of the guests from France were staying somewhere on the premises—in the big house or the guest cottages—which was one of the reasons Jaime and Dom had escaped to an undisclosed inn for the night. Apparently, there was an old-fashioned French tradition of pestering the wedding couple in the middle of the night that Dom didn't quite trust the others not to revive.

Anne slid a glance at Mack, over there talking to Cade, so laughing and relaxed and chocolatey and *alive*, his handprint still on her arm, and her heart started beating so hard she had to slip away.

The caterers and staff could clean up. Anne really had nothing left to do but wash chocolate off herself and tumble into her own bed right next door.

She paused at the archway into her garden, at the sight of Kurt and Kai, with their arms wrapped around each other in a casual, party-worn, chocolatey cuddle. They were staying in the guest cottage on Anne's property, because ever since they got married they preferred having that space of their own rather than a bedroom in the main house when they visited. Even though she had bought that house to make both herself and her son a home.

Kurt was shaking his head.

"But what the hell was Mack Corey doing with his hand on my mom's...my mom's...her..." Kurt gave up helplessly. It was pretty clear he didn't think that any man should be required to fit certain combinations of words together. "She's got a chocolate handprint on her—" He broke off again.

What? Anne slipped sideways so that the rose-covered trellis fencing hid her and tentatively felt her butt, while Kai smothered giggles. Was that hardening chocolate on her butt? Were those the shapes of fingers? He'd copped another feel while he had her down there?

Kai was laughing harder and harder. Anne peered through the roses, the incredulous indignation on Kurt's face more aggravating than comical as far as she was concerned.

Not that she was spying on her own son, of course, but...she just liked to make sure. That laughter, even if she was partly the subject of it, felt so...good. When Anne had given Kai the cabin in the mountains as her refuge, she had never expected Kai to come back out of it with laughter. She'd expected, maybe, for the mountains to eventually release back into the dangerous world a cool, careful replica of Anne herself. Distant. Walled off.

Which would, in some way, have vindicated Anne, confirmed her own choices in life.

It was surprising, still, how glad Anne was to have had, instead, her choices put to question. To see Kurt and Kai find a better path, one where sunlight seemed to spill through the green leaves and bathe them, instead of a high, remote, mercilessly illuminated mountain pass.

"Your mother seemed happy enough with what Mack was doing," Kai pointed out.

What? She *had*? She hadn't seemed cool and tolerant, and slightly ready to hit him?

Kurt gave his wife a perplexed look. "My mom doesn't do that kind of thing."

"Happiness?"

Kurt hesitated and slowly shook his head. "Not really, no. I mean..." He hesitated again, but he clearly couldn't find it in him to say his mother did happiness.

Anne stood very still. This low fist of hurt clenched in her belly. She'd made so much happiness for people. Hadn't she? This wedding, for example. Hadn't that sheltered, nourished happiness? And yet people still sent her to *prison*. Just because they thought she was a cold bitch.

Fuck them.

But she couldn't think *fuck you* at her own son.

She never had been able to grow that cold.

"I don't think she does happiness for *herself*," Kurt said slowly and carefully. "It's the strangest thing. She's afraid of it. So she gives it all to other people."

Kai touched her belly, then caught her hand in the act and shifted it to Kurt's shoulder instead. "It's a beautiful self-protection mechanism," she said softly. "Really, when you think about it, the most beautiful one possible."

Anne took a step back. That fist of hurt in her belly was rising up into her throat, stuffing this stinging sensation toward her nose and her eyes. It didn't feel like hurt anymore, but it felt raw and incredibly painful. As if someone might be trying to force that hurt to unfold its tight fist, and it didn't want to.

"Anyway," Kai said, "she's happy with Mack Corey. Can't you tell? She always has been. He's been her rock for years. Or she's been his." Kai bent her head, and then said low, "You can hurt, and you can handle it badly, and still love someone, you know." She darted a glance up at Kurt.

"Yes," Kurt said very gently, pulling her into his arms. "I do know."

She pressed herself more tightly into his hold. Kurt lifted a hand and petted her blond hair, and they headed on toward the guest cottage.

Anne watched them go, not unhappy, just feeling— ripped apart. Ripped by all that tenderness, by the things they had said.

Nobody had *ever* been tender with her.

An arm settled around her shoulders, firm and warm and entirely intrusive. She barely started. The warmth of it began to seep through her shoulders so fast her reflexes didn't even have a chance to kick in.

"Mack," she sighed in some exasperation, turning her head up to his. He'd run a washcloth over his face and abandoned his tuxedo jacket, but he still retained a fair amount of chocolate damage. Not as much as she did, though, thanks to him.

He grinned down at her. "Chocolate's a cute look on you, Anne."

Oh, for God's sake. "Now I'm cute?"

"Adorable, honey."

Adorable. Honey. "You do know why these heels are called stilettos, don't you? That's what they feel like, stomped into an instep."

He laughed and, without warning, flipped her back against the trellis between two climbing roses, lifting one of her calves up before she even had time to react and pulling off her shoe. "That's one danger avoided." He held it up in front of her nose, grinning at her as he stepped back. Exactly how much alcohol had the man put into his system tonight?

"Mack Corey," she said between her teeth, putting that foot back down on the ground, all lopsided and definitely ruining her fine hose, if that hose had survived the chocolate. "Give me back my shoe."

In answer, he threw it over the trellis, so hard that that she couldn't even hear the thump as it landed somewhere in the distance on her property.

"Better give me the other one now," Mack said. "You'll look ridiculous otherwise. We can pretend you're Cinderella."

About to give in, rather than hobble lopsided all the way to her house, she stopped with her shod foot half-lifted. *"Cinderella?"*

"Well." He laughed. "I admit the humble, submissive, ash-girl wannabe-princess bit is a stretch for you, but *I* could be Prince Charming."

"Mack. I'm pretty sure you couldn't be prince of anything."

He contrived to look genuinely wounded.

Idiot. She rolled her eyes. "It's too low a rank for you." That wasn't obvious?

"Too low a rank for *you,*" he said so casually and cheerfully that it took a moment for the compliment to sink in.

And even then she had to think about it. What did he mean by *for her?* Was he saying she was more than a prince herself, or was he by any chance suggesting that a man had to be better than a prince to deserve her? And if he was, what, exactly, did that mean here?

"I guess that lets out Sleeping Beauty, too," he added. "Despite all the roses." He touched one of the pink ones by her head, stirring their scent in the air.

"Sleeping Beauty was fifteen, Mack."

"Then Prince Charming was kind of a pervert, wasn't he? Breaking into her room and kissing her while she was sleeping. Maybe we should just play ourselves." He gave a shrug of those wide shoulders that always made him look too big for his skin. "*I'm* okay with being *me.*"

What, and she wasn't? She took her other shoe off and handed it to him like a queen to a servant, just to do *something* annoying.

He took it easily in one hand and draped the other arm right back around her shoulders. Damn it. She really needed to find a way to get him to behave, but Mack was notoriously difficult to control and...it brushed across her mind that the angle of her head, right now as she looked up at him, the angle of his, was just like Kai's and Kurt's as they had looked at each other a moment ago.

"I'd better walk you home," Mack said. "The wedding organizer can handle the cleanup part."

"I can get home on my own." Anne brushed her dress. But she didn't twist out from under his arm.

Well...he was warm. The night was getting chilly. In the distance, she could see Kurt and Kai moving behind one of the warm windows of the guest cottage. And in the main house, she could see all the lights she had left on to make a warm welcome home for herself and nobody moving there at all.

"I'll walk you." Mack shrugged. With his arm still across her shoulders, she felt that easy ripple of power in the movement all the way through her body.

It was kind of aggravating. No matter how much power and wealth she amassed for herself and her one heir, she would never be able to impact a man's entire body just by her smallest movement. She would never have been able to flip *him* back against a trellis and steal his shoe before he could stop her.

"There are security guards, Mack."

"I like to see my dates home," Mack said, smugly. "Plus, the state your yard is in, you might bruise a toe and need me to carry you."

The *state her yard was in?* Her immaculate gardens? She gave him her most withering look.

And, as usual, he failed to wither. He rather looked as if he thrived on it. "We can go around the beach way if you like."

It was tempting. The ocean in the dark hours of the night, quiet after the fireworks, waves lapping under the stars. But she didn't have any pockets in this slim dress. She always stuffed her hands in her pockets, when she walked with Mack on the beach in the morning. Suddenly, the inability to do that seemed too— something. The bareness of her arms in the chill, how glad she was for that heat of his arm over her shoulders, the heat of his body against her side. She couldn't go for a walk with him like this.

"I'm tired," she said. Not that she wanted to admit a weakness, but it was better than openly waving a flag of retreat. "I'd just as soon get straight to bed."

"Me, too." Mack grinned, deliberately wicked.

And heat lanced through her again.

She rolled her eyes and headed under the arch. Even though the way she walked did not in the least invite his arm to stay across her shoulders, he managed it anyway, tightening his hold and matching his pace to hers.

He managed that even when she climbed the steps to her front porch. Even when she keyed in her code. "Mack." She sighed, turning. "Look. Tomorrow, I'm going to do you a favor and pretend none of this ever happened."

"Oh, *good*," he said, with a sudden angry, fierce delight, as he dropped her shoe and crowded her right back against her door. "Well, I can do one hell of a lot of things right now, then, if this is all just a fantasy."

And he kissed her.

Just flat out *kissed* her. No careful approach, no slow dip in to make sure she was okay with it, no testing the waters. He just took her mouth and took it over, like she was a damn company and he was pissed off.

Like he was just going to seize all her assets and restructure her.

She felt that way. Seized. Restructured.

His mouth molded hers, dipping straight into hers, his arms tightening on either side of her body until she was locked between his forearms on the door. They pressed against her sides, and then they were curving around her back. And then they were hauling her up into him, as he kept on kissing.

Kissed her until she couldn't think or breathe, until she couldn't get her hands to either pound on him for freedom or grip him to capture this invader and punish him for his invasion.

He kissed her until she was kissing him back, until when he finally raised his head, she had no strength left. What the hell was she supposed to do without her strength? She *always* needed it.

Mack was breathing hard, his face all angles and danger in the lights and shadows of the porch. "Anything else you want to pretend never happened tomorrow?" he asked, with that hushed, wicked *anger*.

She stared up at him, trying to breathe, trying to wet her lips.

"Because I've got a few more ideas."

And suddenly she was so furious she was almost shaking. She could *swear* the fury was why she was shaking. "Go away," she said fiercely and shoved at his chest. "Go away. You're drunk. *Go away.*"

Mack backed a step, his arms falling away to free her. But he didn't stop holding her eyes. "I'm not drunk, in fact. Anne." He reached to touch his thumb to her lower lip.

And that lower lip felt so vulnerable, so exposed and unprotected, that she jerked her head and *bit him*. A fierce, warning nip of the tip of his thumb. "You are, too. If you had to drive home, I'd confiscate your keys and call a taxi. Now *go away*. Before you do something we'll both regret."

He pulled his thumb back to safety. "There's nothing I could do that we'd both regret, Anne."

She folded her arms over her body and glared at him, trying so hard not to shake, trying not to let him see. She hadn't felt this desperate and vulnerable since they'd announced that she'd be spending six months in prison. At least she'd had time to prepare for that. It had been pretty obvious how much everyone in that courtroom but Mack and Kurt hated her and how much they wanted to see her go down. She'd tried to get Mack to force Kurt out of it, so he wouldn't see her as the whole world's goddamn prey, but Kurt, grim-faced, had refused to go.

"Because I wouldn't regret anything," Mack said, and sucked that bitten thumb into his mouth, absently nursing it as he watched her.

"Leave me alone." Anne whipped around and pushed her door open. "Leave me alone, Mack." That was the way she had always been.

"You know, I probably won't do that, Anne," was the last she heard from Mack at her back. "No matter what you say."

She slammed the door behind her.

And for good measure, shot him a bird through the glass pane.

So the last thing she saw as she glanced back was him leaning both forearms against that glass, laughter breaking out on his face, an appreciative gleam in his eye, as she turned and hurried up her stairs.

Was it just her, or did he watch her ass through the glass the whole climb? Because her butt twitched and burned as if he did.

Chapter 7

M ack rolled his shoulders, easing out the stiffness, and threw the worn stick for the dog again. In addition to last night's chocolate wrestling match, he had taken his sons-in-law and Summer's husband to play tennis the morning before the wedding, to try to dissipate their energy before they drove Anne crazy, and also because it was kind of sad seeing a big, bad guy like Dom struggling not to just collapse on the ground and put his head between his knees, hyperventilating. Kid came on all tough when he was facing down a girl's father with his sins in life, the bastard, but he needed to learn how to handle his nerves.

And since he was going to be Mack's son-in-law, Mack figured it was his job to give him a little of the mentoring the man clearly hadn't had from his own asshole of a dad, so...tennis.

As anyone could have predicted, even though Sylvain had played maybe three times in his life and Dom and Luc were barely even aware of what the game was *about*, they still managed to turn it into an intensely rivalrous morning.

Mack, too, of course. Well, shit, he wasn't about to get beaten by his own sons-in-law, when they could barely figure out which end of the racquet to hit the ball with. As usual with rampant beginners, they ran him all the hell ragged chasing their wild balls, until they got into the groove of it, at which point the competition got brutal. Those guys did *not* tire. He wasn't even sure they understood that most human beings sat down and relaxed occasionally.

And hell but Dom did *not* want to lose to Sylvain.

So that had been fun.

His kind of fun, anyway. Everyone had survived it, nobody had literally killed anybody, they'd laughed a lot, and they'd managed to vent a few hours of intense competitiveness. Unfortunately, it had barely taken the edge off the chefs' energy, and they'd still managed to compete all afternoon as to who could make Dom and Jaime the best wedding piece, right in the middle of Anne's professional kitchen next door. Mack, on the other hand, was still sore.

His mouth twisted wryly. Rueful older men had been warning him for decades: *When you're thirty, you're sore for two days. When you're forty, three. When you're fifty...hell, a week, at least.*

He kind of liked it, though. He'd always liked that hint of soreness in his muscles that lingered after he'd really pushed himself. Made him feel alive. Pushing himself was what a man was supposed to do.

The same way that developing Corey Chocolate into the biggest producer of chocolate on the planet made him feel as if he'd pushed himself, or at least flexed his muscles a bit. White knighting for the Firenze brothers and snatching their company out from under Total Foods' nose while Anne was in prison, for example—that had been fun. Total Foods didn't know it yet, but they were *not* getting Europe. *Beat my daughter, did you? Let's see you take on her dad.*

Lex came back panting with the stick, brown ears floppy, shaking water all over him, and he gave the stick another long, hard throw.

And a quiet came onto the beach. A wry, understanding strength. A sense of not being alone. A relief from that solitude he often felt in a crowd, that he often felt even with his own daughters. The dad. The person who was supposed to know what to do.

Well, except now he was leftover. Both his daughters had found someone else.

He nodded at Anne, shoving his hands into his pockets, and kind of wished, for a second, that he hadn't gone so over the line last night. Because what if she—

what if he couldn't talk to her this morning? What if she shut him out? *Could* you break a friendship like this, by being too offensive? God knew, despite all the perverse fantasies he'd had about Anne, she'd never shown much sign of being a sexual being.

He just kind of felt like he could change that for her.

And, *damn*, but he had missed her, when she was in prison. He'd felt as if he'd been broken into a million pieces. It made him *frantic* to put himself all back together again, and fuse her tight into him as he was melding those pieces back, so no one could ever get her away from him again. It wasn't how life worked—they'd gotten to her despite everything he could do the first time—but it was how he *felt*.

Anne nodded to him, too, her hands also in her pockets, and they fell into step, the dog bouncing along beside them from time to time to bring back the stick, Mack throwing it forward. In the morning, Anne always looked like his. No make-up artist polishing her up, whether for a public appearance or on call in the "powder room" she had set up last night so the female guests could stop in for a touch-up. No, in the morning, it was just her skin, dewy from a shower and presumably moisturizer, and some clear, glossy thing she put on her lips. Anne was one of those women who could easily pass for mid-thirties, if she ever managed to carry herself with a little less power and experience. Maybe a Triple AAA personality, sleep-deprived, thirty-something mother of twins some days, but she had these beautiful, elegant strong lines to her bones that were part of the reason she'd done so well on television, and she'd taken good care of her skin and her body. He'd fought the good fight against Botox, when she was tempted in her forties, and won, thank God. *Jesus, woman, why would you want to mess with something that gorgeous?*

Besides, he had a lot of memories held in those fine lines at the corners of her eyes. All those squinting looks across a sun rising over the sea. All those sidelong, minatory glances at something he said. All those times her eyes crinkled in suppressed amusement, laughter dancing in that elusive green. And those newer, tiny vertical lines that tension had left at the corners of her lips—well, he hadn't put them there, but he figured they were his, just the same. He'd liked the way they looked last night, when she was staring up at him on her porch, after he'd given that mouth something better to do with itself than be tense.

They walked in silence, as they often did. Seagulls scattered away as Lex dashed after the stick, with a Lab or an Aussie's energy, although God knew what the dog actually was. Like most of their pets, Lex had appeared on their doorstep in Corey one day, although both the girls had been off to college by the time this particular dog showed up, so Mack had no one to blame for cracking but himself. Brindle brown fur but retriever-shaped, the dog was delirious to be let out now that the bulk of the guests and their no-paw-prints-please reception clothes were gone.

He wondered if Anne had felt like that, when she stepped out of prison. She'd come straight here. Mack had been at the prison with a limo at her release, of course, but she'd been so grim-faced and clearly unwilling to talk yet that he'd left her alone afterward. He knew Anne. It had still pissed him off when he woke up the next morning to find she'd flown off to the Hamptons without even texting him to come with, though. He had flown in after her immediately, to find her already in the ocean. Swimming and swimming in the waves for hours, as if she was going to swim across the Atlantic. Mack had sat on the beach keeping an eye on her, the Coast Guard's number one touch of a call button away, just in case.

Gotten a hell of a sunburn, but then, hers had been worse, out in the water so long after all those months indoors.

"Head hurt?" Anne asked dryly now, at last.

He cut her a glance. A little, amused smile curled her mouth, a woman completely smug about how much of a drunken idiot she *hadn't* made of herself the night before. Probably not the moment to tell her he hadn't had two swallows of that damn champagne. Who the hell had the time, when he was hosting the wedding? Or wanted to dull his brain, when he was challenging Anne Winters?

Except that smug little look on Anne's face pissed him off, and he *wanted* to tell her. Wanted her to know how very not drunk he'd been and that she'd better watch out, because he was *after her* now. His whole body itched with it. What Mack went after, he got.

And his body knew it, too. His body was getting all ready to do every single one of those fantasies in actuality.

"Shoulders," he said instead of any of that, briefly. "I took my sons-in-law out to play tennis, remember?"

Anne smiled a little more. She was a pretty damn good tennis player herself. Competitive as *hell*. She'd hunker down, her racquet ready, and just *grin* as she smashed a shot past him. He'd come so close to locking her up against the tennis court fence and doing obscene things to her when she was all sweaty at the end of some of those matches, she had *no* idea.

A few more steps, another throw for the dog. "How are you feeling?" Anne asked, that quiet tone. Apparently they really were going to let his kisses and his sexual aggression get buried under elegant discretion.

Well, she was going to try that technique, anyway. And he wasn't going to challenge it during their beach walk, of all moments. Some things were too sacred to ever risk disturbing.

Mack shrugged, liking the soreness in his shoulders. "I beat 'em." Answer enough. Anne knew how he liked to win. Especially against competitive, arrogant sons-in-law. Well, Luc wasn't technically his son-in-law, but Summer had such crap-awful parents, he'd always tried to keep up with Julie's habit of including her with his girls whenever possible. Unfortunately, Summer's parents had shipped her off to boarding school right at the same time as Julie died, and Summer had gotten lost there for a while. So had they all.

After a second, he added wryly: "Still paying for it, but I taught them a lesson or two." And after another couple of strides, he had to laugh. "Of course, they didn't know how to play when we started the morning," he admitted.

And Anne laughed, too, that warm, rare, husky sound, kind of like the waves tossing in and the sunlight glancing off them all at once. "'Figure out how you're going to win before you even pick the game'," she told him. It took him a second to remember it was something he'd said once.

Hell, it was one of those things that had somehow gotten quoted in stupid books people read in bathrooms. Nobody cared about his codas, all the times he'd tried to clarify that he actually pretty frequently found himself in the middle of completely new games he had to figure out how to win on the fly.

That was the trouble with being famously successful. Any idiot thought that passed your mind could shape future generations into *deliberate* idiocy, just because they were trying to be you.

"If you get a chance," he said wryly.

Sometimes, after all, the damn Department of Justice took after you, or after your closest friend and ally in the whole damn world, and you couldn't figure out *any* way around those rules, any way to win that game. Fucking bastards.

"Well, you make your chances," Anne said. "But...yeah."

Even though those six months she had spent in prison pissed him off in the worst way possible, he still got a kick out of the way she said *yeah* these days, instead of her elegant *yes*, or just the way she more openly flaunted that *fuck you* attitude. As if under that cool blond exterior, a whole layer of tattoos and piercings was trying to show through. Anne Winters, the elegant, New England punk.

When she'd shot him that bird last night, he'd wanted to suck her middle finger into his mouth and make it feel appreciated.

He'd always known she had that punk part in her, that ability to give a smile that was essentially like raising the middle finger, but he kind of liked her letting the rest of the world see it a bit now, too. Although maybe they'd always sensed it. Maybe that was why the world had gone after her so viciously. *He* could flaunt his *yeah, that's right, I'm smarter, stronger, more powerful than you* attitude openly, but she was a woman, and women weren't allowed to be the strongest person in the room.

Yeah, *fuck you, you pathetic world.* He'd never, ever forgiven it for what it did to Jaime.

Or to Anne.

And it had better leave Cade the hell alone, because that oldest girl of his would kick it in the teeth, if she had to.

"But I meant—you know." Anne waved a perfectly manicured hand. Probably why she'd kept him waiting that morning. Chipped a nail last night and had to repair it before she could take a walk on the beach. It would be like her, but—he'd been getting ready to come pound on her door to make her talk to him again, just in case. "How are you doing. Today. Now that the last one is married."

And his stomach knotted that fast, punched in, closing hard around the loss and emptiness, closing as hard as it could. *Fuck.* He looked away, trying not to let his eyes sting. But they stung anyway. *Shit.* He brought his fingers up to rub them closed, trying to make it look as if he was just having a little trouble with the brightness of the light starting to gleam across the water.

Anne touched his arm. Just that. They'd never walked hand in hand, not ever, but he wanted to link his fingers with hers so bad.

The idea scared him more than all kinds of aggressive come-ons. Anne could roll her eyes over aggressive come-ons, if she wanted. Hell, they could have all kinds of wild sex and still come out of it friends at the end. They'd *taken* hands a few times. He'd gripped hers across a table when it was obvious she was going to lose that battle with the justice system. Held them hard, held her eyes, pushed *you can survive this* into her with all his might. She'd closed hers around his with every muscle in her, when he was on that damn plane flying across the Atlantic to get to Jaime.

But walking hand in hand—that was intimacy. That was a whole different level of vulnerability and softness and shield-lowering.

Still he opened his hand just a little, turning the palm subtly up, making it easy for her hand to slide down his arm and slip right into it, if she wanted.

Hell, he'd raised two little girls and gotten them across all kinds of parking lots, he knew how to get someone to slip her hand into his.

Knew how good it felt when they did.

And how fucking lousy it felt when they didn't. When they grew up and stopped doing that, crossed their own parking lots and looked both ways and didn't need him.

Anne didn't slip her hand into his. She gave his arm a little squeeze and took the wet stick from Lex, tossing it out again.

Then she touched his arm just briefly, delicately again. And slipped her hands back into her pockets.

"It feels like shit," he said.

She grimaced a little and nodded, the wind stirring that pixie cut of hers.

He just wanted to kiss her, okay? Just lean over and kiss her, hold onto her, kiss her some more. Not think about this emptiness his daughters had left. Think about fullness. About all the other things his life could hold.

"But you like them," she said. "Sylvain and Dominique."

Well...like. He grunted. "They're competitive, arrogant bastards."

She raised one eyebrow and slanted a glance at him, her eyes so warm and amused. He did understand why the world called her an Ice Queen, but that warmth of hers—how could it get caught on film over and over, during her shows, and this whole mass of people still not see it?

"So...yeah," he said. "I li—I mean, they're okay. Kind of. I guess."

She smiled.

Like maybe she wanted to lean over and kiss *him.*

Hunh. Really?

"I mean, what the hell my daughters see in them, and why the *fuck* they're so determined to live on the opposite side of the world from me, I don't know." He shoved his hands back in his pockets and scowled at the foam seeping away from his strides, back into the ocean.

Because they had, hadn't they? His daughters. They'd sought out a place as far away from his power over their lives as they possibly could. And it hurt so damn much, he didn't even know how to think about it straight on.

Hell, they liked his *dad.* Their *grandfather* was welcome in their lives. The man who had been the plague of Mack's entire existence.

"I mean—artisan chocolatiers," he said suddenly, and pinched the furrow between his eyebrows, hiding his eyes again for just a second. "I worked so fucking hard. I made—this." He spread his arms out to encompass the ocean and its enormous horizon. Not that he thought he was The Actual God who had created the world—he wasn't that bad, quite—but, you know...close. Corey Chocolate *was* a dominant world player. He had more power than most presidents, and was just as helpless as those guys were sometimes, too. "And they don't even want it. It's like they think it's *crap.*"

Anne's hand came back. This time, she curled her fingers around the edge of his actual hand and squeezed it.

"*Everything* I did for them. My whole fucking life. Every accomplishment. *All* of this. And they don't think it's worth more than some idiot who likes to pretend his little chocolate shop in Paris is the most important thing in the world?"

Anne's fingers flexed again over the edge of his palm. Not quite hand-holding—although, God knew, he made his hand welcoming—but more a nurse consoling a patient. "I don't know," she said, low. A little twisted smile. "Kurt did the same thing, you know. Kai is my polar opposite."

Mack didn't quite know what to say. It stopped him, that different hurt in her. Because he didn't think his daughters had chosen his polar opposite, actually. He and his sons-in-law were a lot alike: the drive, the intensity, the arrogance that made them positive they should be the person controlling any room, their convictions always the most important ones in any space. Fine, yes, he didn't have their fragile, sensitive, princess-on-a-pea natures—nobody could bruise him or pierce him through to the heart just by looking at one of his chocolates askance—but underneath the different accents, they had a hell of a lot in common.

His daughters—well, they'd gone far away physically. They'd done different things with their lives. But maybe, at heart, they actually loved their father a lot and looked for men who were kind of like him.

Hey. Really? His heart warmed all through, this silly, funny, fuzzy warmth that kind of choked him all up, like he'd gotten a teddy-bear stuck in his throat. One of his daughters'. One of those teddy-bears they used to drag along with them when they ran across his office to bury themselves in his lap.

He took a deep breath, letting it out, breathing more sea air in again. Between the memories, and the warm pleasure at the realization that maybe his daughters did get something from their dad, and the loss, it was all—this parenting stuff was a shit hard joy to deal with sometimes.

"Maybe they'll give you grandkids," Anne said, with this strange, wistful wryness. Half humor, half something else. "And your grandkids will rebel against *their* parents and be crazy about you."

Heh. Yeah, and he could drive Sylvain and Dom nuts by luring their children into the capitalist fold. A malicious, delighted curl of his lips at the thought. Nice idea on Anne's part.

Anne.

He frowned. Kurt was a damn idiot, to want someone so different from his mother.

Except—Mack liked Kai. Liked her a lot, actually, this happy, generous-hearted young woman whose eyes lit whenever she looked at Kurt. Kurt and Kai had gone through a real rough spot, but nobody could say that Kurt was an idiot for choosing her.

His frown deepened. After all, if Kurt had chosen someone *exactly* like his mother—that would have been weird, right? Anyway, Anne was a unique challenge. He didn't think most men had the guts for her.

Actually, he was pretty sure only one man in the world had that much guts. And drive. And arrogance. And strength.

He turned his wrist and took her damn hand. Held on to it firmly, too, just in case she got any ideas about using her martial arts training or something to break free.

She started and jerked at her hand.

He slid his fingers down and forced them between hers, locking her hand in tighter.

She stared down at their hands.

He stared right at her face, so that when she lifted her gaze, theirs could lock challengingly. He wouldn't want her to get the wrong idea, after all—like that he might be capable of backing down.

She didn't challenge him, though, when her gaze finally lifted to his. She looked away and bent her head and left her hand in his, all three things which were so unlike her that it hit his heart a little—this startled worry that he might have hurt her somehow in a vital way, or that she might be sick.

"I won't," she said low. "Have grandkids."

And her throat moved, and she bit hard into her lips, and—

Holy *fuck*, were Anne's eyes filling?

Anne was trying not to cry?

Shit.

He just pulled her straight into his arms, wrapping her up hard, holding her close and tight. Two little girls whom he'd single-parented through their teenage years—*yeah*, he knew how hard a girl needed to be held when she was crying. And how long you had to do it sometimes, until they got it all out.

And fuck, the last time one of his girls had gotten badly hurt, he hadn't been *able* to hold her hard. She'd had too many broken bones, and by the time she got well enough for a man to hold on hard to her, she'd already picked out Dom for the job, damn him.

Good guy, though, Dom, in his way. There was that, at least. Mack's hand lifted to stroke Anne's hair—only she didn't have much hair left, of course, unlike his daughters. So he stroked her nape, rubbing it gently while he kept that other arm wrapped tight around her.

"What are you talking about?" he tried roughly, because despite all the lessons from his daughters, he still could not get over that urge to try to *fix* the problem, when the women he loved started to cry. To talk them out of it. To just batter the damn problem to smithereens and make it go away. "Kurt and Kai have plenty of time to still have kids. Lots of couples don't start until their thirties. Hell, Cade's twenty-eight, and no news on that front yet."

Of course, with her living in Paris, he'd probably be the last to know, part of him thought sulkily. She'd probably tell Sylvain, and then her sister, and her sister would tell Dom, and while Sylvain was busy telling *his* parents, she'd be telling Mack's dad next, damn it, because his dad would be over there bouncing around causing trouble and endearing himself to his grandkids like he always did, and her own father would be the very last to know.

"They tried, a lot," Anne told his chest. Her breathing was very funny. Anne hadn't cried for a *prison sentence* and here...surely she was not actually crying? "I think they've stopped trying. The, the miscar—I told you."

The miscarriages, right. Mack was still warily conscious of the fact that he was missing something important here. Were miscarriages *that* hard on people? Like anything you didn't succeed the first time, didn't you just try again?

He tried to imagine what it would have been like for Julie, early in the pregnancy, if she'd lost it, but, God, it had been so long ago. Then he imagined suddenly if Cade or Jaime had never been born and—*fuck.*

Fuck.

Oh, yeah, *fuck* that was a ghastly, god-awful thing to imagine.

Fuck.

His arms tightened around Anne, like he was trying to hold onto his daughters. Or hers, for her.

God damn it, why did the world do this *shit* to the people he loved all the time? This shit he couldn't beat.

"And I never managed to have more kids either," she said, muffled, into his chest. It was so alien to hear Anne's voice muffled, unclear.

Low, quiet, yes. But always clear and firm. Never hidden or protected by anyone's chest. Never protected by anyone at all. She fought her own corners. She defended herself. It was why her walls were so high and strong.

"Shit," he said, because he didn't know what else to say. This was clearly something horribly painful for her that he had never even understood. He petted his hand over her nape again. "Did you—?"

"Oh, yes, I tried," she told his chest. She pulled back, turning away from him. The sudden removal of herself from the hug caught him by surprise, so that she managed to get away before he thought to tighten his arms. "That's more or less what Clark and I broke up over," she said over her shoulder, without really turning her head. A hand came up to dash across her face, at the level of her eyes, but her back was to him and she was already striding away.

He reached out, caught the waistband of her jeans, and yanked her back against his chest. "Sorry," he said, as she fell against him with a startled sound, and he turned her expertly back into his arms—funny how a skill gained from dealing with small girls in a tantrum of tears could come in handy two decades later—and pressed her right back against his chest. "I don't think we were done here."

Broke up, he thought. As if her ex-husband had been some high school boyfriend. Well, that pathetic weak-assed bastard probably didn't deserve the term *divorce*, really.

Even if they had been married over ten years.

Damn, but Mack hated weak men. He couldn't understand them, and how they wasted so many good things just because they were too pathetic to fight for them.

"He got mad at you because you couldn't have more kids?" Clark had cared about kids? The man had moved to California and only seen Kurt during summer visits. Who did that? It wasn't like he lacked for job opportunities closer to where his ten-year-old son lived.

"Nooo," Anne said slowly. She couldn't seem to quite figure out what to make of her forcibly restored position against his chest. She wasn't fighting for freedom, but she wasn't settling in, either. Her fingers, delicate against his chest, couldn't figure out whether to push away or sink in. "I guess it's closer to say I got mad at him. I just—" Her voice tightened all up again, that surreal, unfamiliar tone of Anne fighting tears. "-—it was hard. On me. Not to be able to-to *make* my body carry that little girl I wanted to term. And he—well, he didn't really care very much." And now she pressed her forehead into his chest *hard*, as if she wanted to drive out so many things from her head.

Or maybe just beat down the damn world with her head, and his chest was the closest substitute.

Well, shit. He could be stronger than the wor.d if she needed it. He'd gotten in the habit. It still sometimes managed to win some rounds against him, mostly through sucker-punches, but damned if he would let *it* get in the habit of that.

"I guess they might adopt," Anne said. "I don't know. It's their decision." She shrugged against him, like he was going to believe *that* gesture, and tried to pull back. He let her, a little bit, just so he could see her face. "But if they don't..." She shrugged again, and lifted her chin, and tried that wry smile with which she'd eyed him across the table at the damn courthouse after her sentence came down and they knew she was going to have to do those six months. He'd loved her so much then, for the courage of that wry smile, that it had about killed him. "Well, no grandkids for me."

She stepped away, setting off on the walk again.

He fell into step beside her and looped her back for a hug against his side. "Well, fuck, then, Anne, I guess we'll just have to share mine."

Chapter 8

W hat the hell did that even mean? Share grandkids? Share them how? The way she was Sylvain's "mother-in-law or whatever you call it"? Anne fought the absurd urge to break one of these stupid craft sticks. She usually found it calming, to experiment on her own with crafts for her magazine and show while at the beach, before she got her staff involved in testing the projects. It was why she had this nineteenth-century farmhouse table out on her porch. But today she felt like throwing things.

She couldn't believe how close she'd come to crying in Mack's arms on the beach. What the hell was wrong with her? She didn't cry. What good would it do to show a weakness like that? No one had ever been there to hold her if she did.

Stupid, stupid craft sticks.

She'd only ever started including the children-friendly crafts in her magazine because of Kurt, anyway. She'd liked finding things that made his eyes light up when he was a kid, that combined her life and ambitions with the play and attention he loved, as if they, you know, fit together. As if she was a good mom. Even if she'd screwed up there for a couple of years, when the miscarriages and inability to get pregnant again had hit her so hard, even if she'd divorced his dad and ruined his life, she was still a good mom.

And then it had turned out later that he resented all those hours together crafting and thought she had been forcing him to be her "model crafting child".

Although maybe, still later, he'd come around a bit. As an adult, going through his own devastation, sometimes he would sit and do crafts with her, with a wry, wistful smile.

She sighed.

And then did break one of the craft sticks. Just—snap. It was so satisfying that she broke another, and another, and then as big a fistful of them as she could manage to break at once, frustrated when the resistance wasn't enough.

She threw the damn things on the floor, shoved the rest so that they scattered all over the table, and strode away to her window.

Not her usual view-over-the-beach window. The side one that faced Mack's house.

Red-headed Jaime and her big new husband Dom were in the yard, having come back from their hotel for an extra day after the wedding to be with all the people Mack had flown across the ocean to celebrate with them. Cade and Sylvain were there, too, and a few of those chef couples.

They were getting things ready for a barbecue. Probably there was a text on Anne's phone inviting her over.

She lifted her hands to press against the glass, and there was a rap against the door.

She jumped, turning to find Mack Corey at the top of the outside stairs, with his big hand making a print on her glass porch doors, gazing at her through them.

That was just—she wanted to grab a handful of those broken craft sticks and *throw* them at him. In such a stupid, impotent gesture. All frustration and no will to hurt.

And maybe it wasn't even frustration.

It was—confusion. Restlessness. *Something.* Edgy and tense.

She walked over to the door, so close to growling at him as she opened it that she was surprised her hands didn't form claws.

He gave her that sharp grin of his, the one he usually reserved for opponents, the one that made it look as if he was about to close his teeth around her throat.

96

The one that made her want to bend her head and offer him the back of her neck to rub his teeth over instead.

Maybe he would soften and just rub with his jaw. And her palm itched to lift and test how long it had been since he had shaved, how much it would prickle.

God, she didn't even know how she remembered that a man's jaw *could* prickle. It wasn't as if she had felt a jaw against her nape in...over twenty years.

Since Clark, she had never been willing to trust a man near such a vulnerable spot.

Actually, she hadn't ever really trusted *Clark* near that vulnerable spot. Not once she started feeling vulnerable.

"Ignoring your phone, Anne?"

"I wanted to focus," she said coolly, and his gaze went to the big crafting table and sharpened at all the scattered broken sticks.

He smiled, slow and deep, and stepped inside the house."Me, too. On you."

"Mack." She took a step back, and that pissed her off so much that she clenched her fist loosely to give herself a little more sense of shifting into a boxing stance rather than retreating.

He held his hands up, palm out. "Hey, I kept our walk sacred. I left the sex out of it."

It made her want to *jump* on something, when he said the word *sex*, to stamp her feet like a child in a temper tantrum, only she wasn't sure it was with rage. It didn't *feel* like rage, nor like that concentrated temper in the ring when she went after her opponent. It felt more frantic, more whirling, more incapable of standing still.

And she was the one who could do stillness, who could do coolness. Whose off-camera tendencies to aloof perfectionism had earned her the press nickname Ice Queen.

"Have you been drinking again?"

"I had a beer while I was messing with the grill. Do you know that a group of French chocolatier-pastry chefs who have never grilled a burger in their lives will still find ten ways to suggest a better technique? No, I have *not* tried balsamic vinegar, or bison, or an olive tapenade. And yes, I *do* like mesquite on the flames."

She could see it now. The French chefs crowding around him at the grill, Mack grinding his teeth. The vision was so vivid and funny that just when Anne meant to freeze him out, she had to fight the urge to give him a sympathetic squeeze of the biceps instead. He had fantastic biceps, actually, that his tux last night had covered but that his T-shirt today showed off. "You should have seen them around the wedding cakes. You're getting off easy."

"Ha. So let them do it and see how they like it. Maybe Sylvain will burn off his eyebrows. It might save his life the next time he tries to raise one in that damn—grrr." Mack bared his teeth and curled his hands into a stranglehold shape, clearly not even able to think about the way Sylvain raised his eyebrows without losing speech.

Sylvain Marquis did have kind of a conviction of superiority in that lift of an eyebrow, didn't he?

Of course, he also thought Anne was hot. Anne tried to press down a smug grin at that, and smoothed her skirt. Why she was wearing a skirt in September on the beach, to work in her house, she didn't exactly know. A nice trim one that showed off her butt, too. "I kind of like Sylvain," she said.

Mack gave her a dark, suspicious glance. A—jealous glance? Was that possible? "Damn flirt."

Anne's grin escaped out of her attempts to restrain it. "He does think I'm hot."

Mack's jaw dropped. "That perverted French bastard—he's younger than your son! He's married to my daughter! When did he tell you that?"

"I don't think it was a comment with any actual intent," Anne said dryly. "He wasn't talking to me. In fact, I think he was excusing *your* actions to your daughter."

"I don't need him to excuse my actions, thank you. If he excuses them again, I might have to hit him."

Anne laughed. It felt so new and unfamiliar in her chest, that easy, open laugh. But it just bubbled up. Happy.

Mack stood for a moment stock still just inside the glass doors. "You *like* this," he realized slowly. "Me coming onto you. You don't know what to make of it, but you like it just the same."

Well...yes. Maybe. But that look in his eyes made her want to hold up her hands and back away to the other side of the table. And she wasn't quite sure if it was genuinely to put a barrier between them or because she wanted him to leap over that barrier menacingly and chase her.

"Shit," Mack said, and took a step forward. "All this time..."

Anne did take a step back. And cursed herself. She didn't *retreat*. She never retreated.

Mack's eyes gleamed, old sapphire. He took another step forward.

She took another step back. *Damn.*

She braced herself, determined to hold her ground next time.

He took one more step forward, and she managed it, she held up her chin and dug in and locked eyes, and didn't step back. Which brought him right up close to her, his finger lifting to trace the hollow of her throat. "You want to know how much I had to drink last night?" Mack asked, in that rough voice he had sometimes after three days of meetings as he negotiated a buyout.

Anne half shook her head, then remembered she was supposed to nod. But...she wasn't entirely sure she did want to know.

"Maybe three sips." His hand followed that curve at the base of her throat. Back and forth. Thumb stretching up to stroke that soft, vulnerable skin. "I tried, don't get me wrong. But at first, every time someone would thrust a glass of champagne in my hand, I'd make a toast, there'd be pictures, and then, before I could even drink the damn thing, someone would grab me for something else. And later I...didn't want to lose my focus."

And those blue eyes *focused*. Right on her. Like a mastiff focusing on a rival it had to beat.

Anne tried to narrow her eyes at him. "So, what then? You just lost your mind under the stress of being father of the bride?" The man who never caved to the stress of international business negotiations?

"I didn't lose my mind. My mind just kind of woke up and focused. It's amazing how effective a dash of cold water on a man's dick can be at reaching to his brain. And I realized I should trust you."

What?

Why did that sound so—strange? Opposite? That *he* should need to trust *her*?

"I mean, twenty years, Anne. If you want to knee me in the groin or slap me or say yes, if we have good sex, or crappy sex, or no sex, any way this can go, I'll still be on that beach tomorrow. Won't you?"

She sighed very heavily. "Of course I will, you idiot."

A smile around the edges of his mouth, tight and happy and carefully contained. But his eyes were brilliant. "So I can't lose you. And that's the only thing I've been afraid of. What about you? What are you afraid of?"

She stared up at him. It was hard to breathe, the hair on her body rising as if it wanted to reach him while her body held still, afraid. But she couldn't stand to lie to him. If she couldn't tell the truth to Mack—who was left? Certainly not herself. He *was* her truth. What let it come out. Like a prism revealed a rainbow. "Of letting you in," she finally managed, almost inaudibly. Yes.

Exactly that. Of letting him in where he could hurt. Where he could disappoint. Where he could betray.

His big hand, with the little calluses from squash and golf, rubbed down lower until it lay just over the swell of her breast. "I'm not already in?" he asked softly, puzzled and on the borderline of hurt. The heel of his palm nudged against her chest, the words unspoken: *In there?*

Her heart thumped, thumped, thumped against his palm. The strong cords of his throat were just on level with her gaze, the tan from all that beach walking and golf, the lines from half a century of strength. The gray prickle starting to show on his jaw. Ah, yes, then, if he touched his jaw to her nape, it would prickle. The thought of it hummed down her spine.

"I—am I in yours?" she asked, as if it was this great daring question, as if she was afraid, and that was *inane* when she heard it out loud. Of course he cared about her. He'd fought like a lethally intelligent pit bull for her. He'd walked in quiet with her. He'd...been there.

Mack shook his head, those lines that time had started to grow on his forehead deepening. "Anne." He opened his hand, so utterly baffled by her question. "You know how Julie used to wear that charm bracelet, with a precious stone for me, and one for each of the girls? If I had one of those, I'd have Julie." He rubbed his thumb and index finger together, against his wrist, as if he was rubbing a bead on a bracelet. "Hers would be beautiful and all worn, from time. Faded. But I'd like having it there, to rub. It would reassure me. And I'd have my daughters. Those ones would be so bright and beautiful, the most vivid, rich colors. Murano glass, maybe, red and blue. I'd have my dad." A little smile. "He'd be all poky and pointy, aggravating my thumb." His smile faded into puzzled, searching seriousness. He opened his hand. "And I'd have you."

Her throat choked up so hard until it was all she could do not to cry. Her chest hurt. As if some great carapace of ice, thickened through many winters, was being broken off it, piece by stubborn piece. "What—what color would I be?"

His fingers flexed into his palm. "The closest I could get to that first gleam of light across the waves when the sun slips over the horizon. Almost no color. Just glow."

It was so hard not to cry. She didn't fight the tears because she was afraid of what *he* would do, if she cried. She fought them because she was afraid that if she started, the size of that cry would rip her apart.

That was all that was left of her was a carapace, right?

What would she be if some damn flood of tears melted it away?

She backed away again, and his gaze flared as it held hers, and then just—*locked.*

"I can't," she whispered.

His mouth compressed, and anger glittered a second in his eyes. "Can't you?" Danger there.

She liked it. Liked it with the beating, hungry fear of a queen looking down from the ramparts that had walled her in so long at the armored king who had lined his forces up against her. *He could win this. He could tear them down.*

"I have to fight." Broad daylight, just the two of them, and she could not get her voice above a whisper. She backed again, aiming for the table, to put it between them.

His body grew tenser, stronger, that flare in his eyes vivid and dangerous. Mack liked to fight. He was very, very good at it.

So was she.

"I can't—I *have* to fight."

Help me. Let me fight.

His fingers curled into his palms, these hungry, half-fists. Not full fists. Because they didn't want to hit, they wanted to grab.

She had built those walls for so long. From inside them, they looked impenetrable: white and smooth and thick, the treacherous, cruel world so far away. That world she didn't trust, for good reason.

But *he* could break them down.

He took a step after her.

Her teeth bared a little, energy surging in her as it did when she pulled on her boxing gloves, but so much better, more scared, more intense, and her hands lifted.

"Be careful, Anne." His voice was the gravel of a battering ram being dragged into place. "Trust me, I've had plenty of fantasies where we fight. And I always win."

Her lip curled, her blood pumping. "You think so?" But she wanted him to win. Behind those walls, she was terrified he would lose. Everyone else always had. Without her even getting a chance to flex her full strength in the battle. Like a wisp of clouds, those other men. They brought up their forces, they pretended to lay siege, and she took a deep breath in preparation for battle—and at its release, they just dissipated.

Hopeless, stupid illusions with no strength.

Mack knocked her hands aside, grabbed the two panels of her tailored white shirt, and ripped them open.

Buttons flew. She gasped, her heart pounding in shock and agonized delight as he tore that outermost wall apart and left her naked.

"I know so. I've been practicing this one in my head a long time." His teeth showed, the promise of a bite. "I know every single move you might possibly make. And what to do about it."

"You don't know the version where you lose," she flung back at him. Her teeth showed, too.

"That's because that's not a possible outcome." He took another step into her, forcing her back against the wall. His chin jerked at her hands. "Go ahead, Anne. Hit me."

Damn it, she couldn't. She didn't want to hurt him. "Fuck you."

"No, you," he said, with those glittering, beat-the-world eyes and that battering ram voice. "Isn't that what we're talking about?" His voice went low, low, low, so deep it vibrated through her bones. "Fucking you."

Her fist flew out—toward his chest, a completely safe target. No way she could really hurt him there. Almost no way she could hurt him anywhere with a punch now, his closeness stealing all her power. She'd have to duck and slide away, give herself room to maneuver.

He grabbed her wrist and forced the hand that had hit him back against the wall.

Her whole body responded to that, in one swirling heat of arousal. *Oh, God, what if he actually gets through? We'd better get ready.*

The preparation for defeat pressed against her breasts until they were maddeningly desperate for contact to relieve them, made her sex clutch vainly on emptiness.

"Fucking you every way I want to." That deep vibration spread out from her bones through her whole body. Vibrating mercilessly in every erogenous zone. "That's a lot of ways, Anne."

She punched him in the stomach. Knowing the range limited her, knowing that even with all her strength in that shortened punch it wouldn't be enough to hurt.

He tightened his stomach to receive it, those hard muscles all the shield he needed. His body crowded her even closer against the wall as he caught that wrist, too, his thigh between hers, pressing her up, leaving her no room even to go for his groin. The best her hips could do was bump and grind. *Good.* So she did that. She did that *as if* she was fighting to do worse, and he grunted with the pleasure of it, his hips pressing back.

Every single thing about him was bigger than her. Bigger in height, bigger in the shoulders, bigger in strength, all dominating hers now. She hated how much he outmatched her, but it was so glorious. *He might actually win.*

"Anne." Imperious, his voice commanded her attention. Like an emergency call, breaking into a studio session. Like something urgent had come up, and he needed to get through.

She wanted to *bite* him when he said her name like that. Her hips bucked for it, trying to lift her toward his mouth.

His eyes held hers, mercilessly blue. "How am I supposed to know if you really want me to stop?"

Her energy deflated. She should have known it would be that easy to beat him, even him. That easy to stay behind her walls. "I'll tell you to stop." She turned her head away in defeat. Just one word, then, was all it would take, to keep those walls strong. *Damn him.*

A hard hand released one wrist to take her chin and force it back to face him. His head lowered closer to hers. Not like the promise of a kiss. Like the threat. "What if I cover your mouth with my hand so you can't?"

Arousal raced back through her, a giddy and disorienting hope. "I'll bite you."

His voice grew even rougher, deeper. His body pressed harder. "What if I like it?"

She sneered at him. Sneered at herself. "Then I'll cry." As if she would ever cry. That morning on the beach when she had come close had been so bad—that painful, raw feeling of arms holding her at her weakest, of being *loved.*

But that would definitely stop him, if she cried.

His mouth came so close it nearly brushed her cheek, just under her eye. His voice was not even sound, just a gravel breath: "What if I just lick away the tears?"

Her body jolted against his. That sudden vision of such sweet, carnivorous intimacy.

He pulled back, his teeth sharp. "I need more salt in my diet."

She stared at him, energy thrumming through her, thrumming and thrumming, as if her whole body was the body of a guitar. She reached up a hand and seized him by the neck as if she wanted to shake him. "You're going to eat my tears?" she demanded between her teeth.

He shrugged. "If they taste good."

Her nails sank into his neck, and she *yanked* his head down to her, yanked herself up into him when he didn't yield fast enough, and she *bit* a kiss onto his mouth.

Bit hard. Bit deep. Sank her tongue and her lips into it, gave it fury. *There. That will teach you to kiss me like that last night. That will—*

Teach you.

He learned fast. Twisting that kiss back around on her, taking *her* mouth with teeth and tongue until she could barely breathe, and when he lifted his head she sank panting against the wall.

He braced himself on his forearms, his weight heavy against them, barely held off her. He was breathing hard, too, his lips damp and a little swollen. "So how am I supposed to know?" he pressed at her.

She nearly growled at him, her teeth bared. "I'll scream for the guards! And have you arrested." Was that good enough? They both knew she would never do that to him.

The way they both knew he would never do anything bad to her.

And yet still she had to fight. She *had* to. If she could have just walked out from behind those walls, she would have done it long since.

"But what if I do this?" His hand slid fast down to the hem of her skirt and pulled it straight up, pressing his hot palm into her panties.

Anne went very still. She couldn't even remember what it felt like to have a hot palm pressed between her legs. This wild, burning paralysis that came from it, that swept through her body.

His voice went very low. The heel of his palm nudged insistently. "Then what are you going to do, Anne?"

She shook her head mutely. Her breath grew too shallow, dry, ragged sips of air.

"Nothing?" he murmured, his eyes gentling, even as his body hardened still further. He rubbed her through her panties. "You like that, Anne?" His voice had gone— tender. Possessive. Insistent.

She angled her head away.

His voice dropped nearly beyond sound, just a fierce breath of satisfaction. "Ah, you do."

No, she didn't. She couldn't like something that was driving her crazy.

His voice deepened further, more intimate, caressing, his mouth coming close to her ear. "Would you like it right here?" He kept rubbing so gently and relentlessly, his body closing all around hers now, hiding her in him. His mouth touched her earlobe. His jaw prickled down her throat. "I've thought up well over fifty ways to make you my lover."

"'Leave,'" she managed, barely a breath. The feelings that were climbing through her from his hand were too strange. Someone else's hand didn't give her those feelings. Not ever. "It's fifty ways to *leave* your lover."

"Yeah, I don't do that leaving shit." His prickly jaw trailed down her throat. "If you haven't figured that out about me yet, Anne, you haven't been paying attention." His hand rubbed, experimenting, testing pressure to see what made her shiver. Testing rhythm. He bit her shoulder, gently. Her bared shoulder. That's right, she was stripped down to her bra and ripped-open shirt.

"Mack. I just—" She turned her head into his neck, closing her eyes. "It's just—please, I—" Had she said *please*? She didn't beg.

"Do you want me to tell you some of them?" That deep, rough voice rubbed itself against her throat as it somehow managed to vibrate all the way down the core of her body and stroke between her legs.

She tried to hold still, because she didn't know how to let what was happening to her be *seen*. The blurring, trembling heat coming up from his hand through her body.

"That table," Mack said. "Right there. That heavy, old table with its wood all worn to silk, that you like to run your hands over. I've thought about pushing you back on it and spreading your legs while you say *no* and putting my mouth to you until you say *yes*."

Her body liquified, and that liquid crept out through her panties and bragged about itself.

"Ah, you like that one." That rub of his hand was a rub of approval. "And then eventually you beg, in that one. You grab at me, while you say, 'Fuck me, fuck me, Mack, *please*.'"

God. Her hands dug their way up his arms, begging for support.

"That's a good one," he said. "I have that one a lot. And then there's the one where you look at me over your shoulder, trying to freeze me. Only *I* have the magic power, of course, and I just snap my fingers, and all your clothes melt away. And there you are, still looking at me. But you're all naked, Anne. Your back, your butt. And I can just walk up to you and stroke my hands wherever I want, all over you, until—once again—you're begging, and twisting, and just incoherent with want. I don't think you can even manage to say *fuck* in that one. It depends on the night."

Her skin felt tight, need and desire tightening and tightening in her, drawn into his hand, until everything, everything about her entire being depended on that rhythm. That sound of his voice, reverberating through every intimate part of her body.

"And then there's this one," he murmured.

108

Her head sank onto his shoulder, her mind hazy, full of words and images and the rub of his hand.

"This one right here." His voice sank through her. His hand rubbed.

"The one that starts just...like...this." His thumb twisted where his palm had rubbed, and she arched into him suddenly, her nails digging, the heat exploding into her, up from his hand. This surprise assault. A series of explosions that kept coming, that one big shocker, and then more and more little ones, as if the attack would never end.

Pleasure bombarded her and wouldn't stop. So much pleasure it made her want to collapse before it and just weep from it. But there were too many shocks of pleasure to leave time for tears.

She hid her face in his shoulder while he rode them, while he kept his hand gentle and persistent until he'd milked the last one from her and then they all slowly faded away. Even after her body finally calmed, she still kept her face hidden in his shoulder, no idea what expression to put on it when she lifted it.

He picked her up, pulling her thighs apart around his hips, pressing his own jean-clad arousal into her wet panties. "And then," he said. "Then there are the fifty or so with the bed."

Chapter 9

He tossed her on the bed like his spoils from a war. She bounced on the antique white linens and scrambled to get up on her elbows, even as he landed in a sitting position on the edge of the bed beside her and thrust his arm between her legs so they couldn't close against him.

"A.L.W." With his other hand, he traced the monogram she'd had added to those old linens and showed his teeth again, in that fierce, hungry victory. "I'm glad you told me whose bed this was, Anne, so there wouldn't be any confusion about whose territory I'm taking over. You want me to give you some new sheets that say M.A.C.?"

Just the thought both shot arousal through her again and made her want to strangle him for his gloating, subdue him under her. Teach him who was queen here.

And yet his forces were already well inside her walls.

"Mack." She grabbed for verbal weapons. "I don't have any—there's nothing in my nightstand, you know."

"Anne." He braced his hand against the great oak headboard behind her. Victorian. She'd painted it white herself. White on white everywhere here. Untouchable. Aloof. "I haven't had sex with anyone but you in a long, long, long time."

"You haven't been having sex with me either!"

"It's been vicarious." He pulled a packet out of his back pocket. "But I brought some anyway. In case you felt fastidious." He waved the foil packet at her and gave that little, mean, I'm-beating-you grin. "Make you mad?"

That he had come assuming he would win? Yes. She pressed her lips together and glared at him.

He leaned forward until he pressed his hands to the mattress to either side of her face, his thigh sliding up between her legs. "Enough to say *Fuck you?*"

"F—" She caught herself and tightened her lips again

"I brought three," he taunted, pressing his thigh right up between her thighs and rubbing it there. "Go on, Anne. Say it."

Again the provocation nearly brought the words out. She fought them back.

"God, you're so mean," he said and lowered his hips enough to drag the fastening of his jeans between her spread legs, a masculine, rough invasion between her thighs that was *nothing* like anything she could ever give herself. "Me, too."

She gave a little hitch of breath as he rocked his hips just an inch or two back and forth, dragging the thick placket of his jeans against her.

"You can either say that or *fuck me*," he told her. *My way or...my other way.*

"Or you could say it," she shot back, even as her hips rocked up into him for more of that maddening, *invasive* masculinity.

"Oh, yeah, sure." He pulled down her panties, his fingers sliding in against her sex as if they had an incontestable right to do whatever the hell they wanted with her. "Fuck me, Anne. Fuck me out of my mind." Two fingers drove straight into her sex.

Into.

Her sex.

Into her.

He was in her.

And he *liked* it. His face was fierce, gleeful, triumphant.

"Now, see," he said. His fingers moved deeper. "Now I can say I've fucked you. Whatever else happens, I'll have fucked you with my fingers, Anne." His fingers eased up. Plunged back in deeper. "I've gotten *in.*"

"You bastard." Her inner muscles tightened around him, and she barely even knew she *had* inner muscles. She used them for pelvic exercises. That was all. She did them the same way she had microdermabrasion done from time to time and always made sure to use her facial creams. To stay perfect, in health, beat age, not find herself wearing a diaper thirty years from now. She didn't use them *for sex.*

But now she did. Tightening on him, grabbing for those fingers slipping out. Lifting up to seek more of them, until he gave that victorious, smug, damn *fierce* grin and drove them right back in.

He bent his other arm, bringing his weight onto his forearm, his body just above hers, pinning her, as he kept up the motion. "Want to be fucked with anything else?" he whispered, tauntingly.

Yes. Damn him.

Damn him for her hero. Mack Corey, you goddamn conquering warrior king. Why didn't you attack years ago?

But then again, why hadn't she thrown him a rose down from her tower or something? Or just opened the damn gates and let him in?

Maybe she'd needed to be dragged out of her castle into someone else's prison to shake her up, to give her the guts or the temper. The struggling, kicking, screaming, panicked courage.

"Or do you want to *fuck me*?" he whispered into her ear.

"It's the same thing," she managed, even as her hips bucked.

He shook his head. "It's a completely different perspective." Just like that, he rolled them so that she was astride him.

She gasped at the exposure and vulnerability, her skirt bunched up all around her, the panels of her shirt flapping. Involuntarily, she tightened her stomach muscles. What she looked like from this perspective hadn't been an issue since...well, since she had been young enough that it also hadn't been an issue. Even when she was fighting her stomach muscles back into shape after Kurt's birth, she'd only been twenty-one, so those muscles and skin had still cooperated then with her drive for perfection.

She had no idea what she looked like from Mack's point of view, but she knew what he looked like from hers.

At her mercy.

The man who had come to attack her castle had been captured by its queen.

Oh, yeah. She could get used to this.

She pinned his wrists.

That was ridiculous, her fingers only half closed around them. But his eyes glittered up at her, as if she had him trapped. His hips bucked up against hers.

Now *she* rubbed *him*—rocking her pelvis forward and back, dragging her sex against his jeans.

Mack's breath came in harshly. "They unzip, you know."

"Maybe you should beg," she retorted, her chin up loftily, her heart pounding. Her whole *body* pounding. With him. With that want for him. For so much more than her life held.

His eyes glittered, willing victim. It was a trap. He was luring her in. No way *Mack* would be willing to lose. He arched his head back, exposing that strong, tan throat. "Fuck me, Anne," he pleaded in a whisper, as if his throat was all parched, as if he was desperate in her prison. "Come on. Fuck me." His hips pressed up again.

She pulled her torn shirt off, because it was getting the hell in her way, and threw it onto the floor. A long breath moved through his body, his eyes brilliant blue. The light fell through her pale, transparent curtains, onto him. Breeze stirred over them, that cooling September wind off the sea.

"Do it." His hips pressed more insistently. "Come on, Anne. Take at least one piece of my goddamn clothing off."

She considered him for a long moment, enjoying the way she could torment him just by barely twisting her hips. Torment herself. Then, still astride him, she leaned over to her nightstand drawer and pulled out her tiny embroidery scissors. Mack's eyes widened at the sight of them, and he held very still, as if he might be genuinely afraid her instincts for torture were going to come out. As if he felt genuinely caught at the mercy of a dangerous queen.

She smiled at him, in sweet, mean reassurance, writhed her pelvis down hard against his as she leaned in, and brought the tiny lethal scissors right up to his throat. His lips pressed tight together as he held his breath.

She opened the scissors with a little snip, holding his eyes. His flinched a little and then locked hard with hers. He pressed his fists on the mattress where she had left them, as if she'd locked them there, not grabbing her wrist or knocking those scissors away from his throat.

Very carefully, she cut through the hem of his T-shirt's neckline. His breath left him in a little gasp. Then she set the scissors back on the nightstand, grabbed either side of that cut, and ripped the panels in half.

"Holy shit." Mack's breathing had gone ragged. "Oh, shit, *fuck*, that's hot. Anne. Anne, honey. Come *on.*" His hips bucked again.

She drove her own pelvis back down onto him with all her force, trying to master his hips with hers. But of course, his just fought back, both of them driving against each other in this contest of grinding strength that made his cheeks flush and his chest lift and fall harder and harder.

She pushed the panels of his shirt fully aside and studied that chest as its muscles flexed with his breaths.

Damn, he had a nice body. Those broad shoulders, tanned from all those ocean swims, and that hard chest. Fifty-three years of confidence, experience, work. His body knew damn well who he was and what he could do about it.

She ran her hands over it, suddenly, utterly— *delighted*. Happy. Not afraid. Not fighting. This heat under her hands, this strength—

She didn't even know she had the word *wow* in her vocabulary.

And yet it was—*Wow*.

Incredible, spectacular, delicious. All that under his T-shirts when he walked beside her on the beach, all this time?

It was hers to *touch* now?

It was so *warm*.

Like touching some sun-wolf or something. She bent down and pressed her lips there in that hollow of muscle where his shoulder turned into his chest.

Then she sat right back up and raked her nails, delicate and dangerous, over the spot.

Mine. See what happens when you try to attack my castle?

His eyes gleamed up at her as if he knew now exactly the error of his ways. But, bizarrely, he didn't seem afraid.

He seemed pretty damn full of himself, to be honest.

His hands went of their own accord to the button of his jeans.

She let them. She liked the way his knuckles bumped and ground against her sex while he fought with the button. She even twisted her hips to put that bump and grind into just the spots she wanted it.

"Come on," he begged again for mercy. "Come on, Anne, let me get my—" He managed to slide the zip down, so that his penis sprang up against her, blocked only by soft cotton briefs.

She smiled, a smile that felt slow and mean and silky, and very deliberately, very gently, rubbed herself against that penis, dampening that cotton, making it cling to him. And to her. She wanted to thrust herself onto him just like that. Just grab him, cotton and all, and wedge him inside her.

But when she reached for him—well, it was so much simpler to thrust that underwear out of the way.

He twisted his hand and cupped her, blocking her sex from his in the most pleasurable way possible. "Just a second. It's been a while since I've had to use one of these things." As he twisted away from under her body to rip open the packet, he offered a wry grin. "Had to watch a YouTube video to make sure there hadn't been any advances on the best method since the last time."

He'd laid his practical groundwork that carefully? Oh, of course he had. Mack never lost a battle just because he'd failed to get all the information he needed.

It was so *lovable,* the caution with which he put the condom on. Not unconfident, but paying attention to make sure he got it right. Not something he could do without thinking.

How long *had* it been since the last time he'd had to use a condom? She hadn't seen him with another woman in a long, long time. Mostly he seemed to date her, their "dates" to charity dinners and other functions. Nor did he ever talk to her about anyone else, except when he asked for her help fending off a particularly insistent young woman after his money. And Mack talked to her about pretty much anything.

"Hurry up," she said. "Or I'm going to have to do it for you. And I haven't been checking YouTube."

"'Hurry up'," Mack murmured, with that deep, savoring tone. "That's *almost* like *fuck me.* Only with huge room for erotic improvement. Come on, Anne." He rolled back under her, but when she would have settled cautiously back into the position for which she'd been so hot before the interruption, he grabbed her hips and held her off. That fierce, taunting grin. *Ha, I've got control again.* "Say it."

"Mack." She tried to twist her hips down against his grip. Big, dominant hands tightened. "You bastard."

He smiled, with complete lack of apology. "I know."

"There's no need to be proud about it!" Again she tried to twist down toward his penis. Again, he just held her, taunting and victorious.

"I am, though," he said. "People always call me that when I'm about to beat them." He lowered her hips just enough that his erection grazed her sex. She drew a hiss of breath.

So did he.

But he didn't break for all that. He controlled her hips and his, shifting them enough to moisten his length against her sex.

She bit her lip, as the need for more washed through her, as her head arched back.

"You could always say it," Mack whispered his taunt. "Then I'd do it."

"Mack," she said between her teeth, straining between need and rebellion. "Fuck you!"

"Close enough. That was my second favorite." And he pulled her hard and sure right onto him. Just—bam.

Anne drew a great, shivering gasp. For a second, she could only sit, impaled on him, astride. So ridiculous, so vulnerable, so exposed. So *invaded.*

He stared back up at her, frozen, too. Their eyes held, and he licked his lips, his chest lifting in one huge, shuddering breath. "Anne."

She closed her eyes.

He jostled her with his hips, sending sensation washing through her. She hadn't let anyone inside her in so long, she'd forgotten there was even a way in. And here he was. *In.* Deep and hard and sure.

And her body kept clutching around him, tightening and flexing in this frantic motion, as if it was trying to close over the hole he made. Only he wasn't about to remove himself and let it.

So her flexing, frantic muscles flexed around him.

And God, but he liked it.

He shuddered, arching his hips up into her. "Oh, shit, Anne, please do that again."

So—yeah. She did. Again. And then again, as color suffused his face, as his fingers dug into her hips, as he lifted himself up against her, as he fought her for the rhythm.

Hey. This was *fun*. Giddily, erotically delightful.

She leaned down over him, pressing her forearms against his shoulders and chest as she rebelled against the rhythm his hands tried to impose, setting her own pace.

He groaned.

Yeah, this was really fun.

Malcolm Anthony Corey. In her power.

It might even be that the tiniest movement of her body could be felt all the way through his.

She went very still on him, so that his eyes popped back open, and his hands gripped her to try to get her moving again. Instead, she gave just a little squeeze of her inner muscles.

He flinched and groaned and shoved his hips up for more.

She grinned.

His eyes narrowed menacingly, which was hilarious, really, given how vulnerable he was to her. "Anne, you—"

"What?" she taunted merrily. Energy zinged through her. Sun-filled. Happy. Hungry.

He brought his hand between them. "I think I need to bring another weapon into play."

She gasped as his thumb touched her already super-sensitized clitoris. Her movements slowed, as the sensation from it washed through her, more powerful even than the sensation of him inside her, or maybe working in tandem with it. Maybe it was all too powerful. Too much.

"Mack," she whispered, as her eyelids closed out the world, everything but those feelings.

"Don't worry, Anne, I'm going to," he promised to everything she couldn't say.

"Going to do what?" she managed to challenge. Because she still just had to challenge.

"Every single thing I can think of. Or that you can. Just give me your next fifty years."

She drew great breaths, not sure what to say, not even able to open her eyes. She'd been going to give him her next fifty years anyway. Just—without the sex. Without *this* much warmth and love and vulnerability.

He rolled them over, his body coming up to dominate hers, to take all the power again. "Oh, and—say it," he breathed to her. "Then I'll do anything you want."

Her eyes flared open.

His were always so damn blue. But this time, under the dark gray eyebrows, in that tan, time-marked face, they were blazing.

"You bastard," she told him weakly.

He kissed her, his tongue slipping deep into her mouth, stealing that word right back out of it. "Come on, Anne."

She wrapped her arms around his neck and pulled herself in close to his ear. "Fuck me," she whispered. "You happy?"

He grinned in utter triumph. "It lacked conviction. We might have to practice it some more. That's okay, honey. I've got some ideas about how."

And he let them both go. All words gone, driven out by the rhythm. His face dark, everything drawn into the pleasure, in her, his thumb against her, until she clawed his back in her fight not to come again. It scared her, it was like a tsunami wave, she clawed to get away. But she lost, it overtook her, she drowned in it, as he drove into her one last time and held on, swirling away in it, too.

Chapter 10

Mack was about as full of himself as a man could be. He felt like marking some victory brand on his skin with the tip of his sizzling finger. *Score five million for me.*

Score everything.

Shit, hell. Anne Winters! He'd gotten Anne!

He filled up her great whirlpool bath and put her in it while he took a fast shower, far too invigorated to laze around.

"I'm sore," Anne told him, when he asked her when she wanted to get out. "Go away." But she was smiling a little when she said it, not quite looking at him, but not looking away. A little...shy? Happy? Ruefully self-conscious? He might have to learn a whole new range of expressions for her.

This one reminded him of nothing so much as a kitten his girls had had, the first time it had managed to sneak through the door outside, stopping still, its eyes going big, its paws cautious, easy for Jaime to scoop back up and bring back inside.

A cautious kitten? Anne Winters?

And yet it was so oddly appropriate. *The world looks bigger outside that castle, doesn't it, kitten? I bet you'll take to it really fast, though.*

Shit, he hoped so.

"Come on, Anne, you can't tell me that was worse than one of your boxing sessions."

"It's not the same muscles," she said very loftily and coolly, and he just leaned over the rim of the big bath and kissed her.

She caught her breath at the contact of his lips, and a flush climbed her cheeks.

He grinned. *Yep. See? That's what you just did. You let me in. Now I get to kiss you as much as I want to.*

Unless...well, unless she did say *no thanks*. Unless they went back to just the beach walks.

He sat on the edge of the bath now, and took her hand, joy fading a little before seriousness. Would she do that?

That'd be crappy. He hadn't quite realized how crappy it would feel ahead of time, to have gotten in, and then get kicked back out. He had a *hell* of a lot more fantasies to get through, but it wasn't just that.

There was a trust thing going on. Damn it, he liked fighting, but he wanted to be able to curl up on the couch and cuddle. He wanted to hold hands. Yeah. He wanted someone to just slip her hand into his as natural as breathing, as if that was the best place in the world for her hand to be. He wanted her to come to Paris with him and turn that damn, sterile luxury apartment he and his dad had bought into something welcoming, a second home.

She'd probably fix his apartment up for him anyway, if he asked her, and buy another one for herself while she was at it. The woman had a home-buying addiction. But...he wanted her to be *inside* the cozy home she made, part of it. With him. A cozy home with nobody but himself and his dad rattling around inside it wasn't cozy at all. It had no future, a home like that. It became a place where a man didn't savor the prime of his life, he just dwindled into lonely old age.

Well, hell, if she did kick him back out, he'd just have to keep working at it from another angle, wouldn't he? Give her a break to get used to it. To miss it, maybe. Come around again from the flank.

It was like anything you wanted to get in life. Even when things seemed to be going well, you plotted for every eventuality and figured out how to win at every single one of them.

"I'm pretty sure Sylvain and Dom have ruined those burgers by now," he sighed.

She covered her face with her free hand and started to laugh.

His grin came back. This was going to work out. He might not even have to keep fighting the battle for a couple of years before it did, either.

And what was he doing wasting this moment because he was so full of himself he couldn't sit still? If he wanted a cuddle...no time like the present.

He shrugged the guest robe back off, trying not to wonder whether it was just one of those things Anne automatically kept around, the way she had everything always exquisitely prepared for any possible guest, or whether it had ever been worn by any man but him. If it had, she hadn't ever let him even realize the man existed, which meant it probably wasn't his business. He gave the thing a little kick when it dropped on the floor, though, just in case.

The weirdest feeling flashed across him as he slipped into the bath with her—he was almost self-conscious, too. Just for a second, he thought of all the younger men who had pursued Anne. His own damn son-in-law thought she was hot, the bastard. Mack had a strong body. He felt good in it and treated it well, gave it exercise, took it outside to live. But just for a second, he thought of the cocky twenty-somethings she could have instead, if she wanted. That tight feeling he'd had to his skin back then, that suppleness to his every movement, that a man fresh out of college took for granted.

Anne looked up at him as he climbed in, and her eyes widened and widened. Damn it, she really did look like that kitten.

Yes, here we both are, naked in a tub. Naked together. That's how this works, Anne.

Hell. This was going to be a *lot* trickier to maneuver than fight-sex. Anne *loved* to fight. Who didn't?

But being vulnerable and naked...yeah, that was a lot harder.

"Don't you need to get back to the barbecue?" Anne asked uncertainly. Not quite fighting him off snappily, but not exactly relaxing her guard, either. Yeah, inside the castle, there were all kinds of musketeers ready to spring to the queen's defense.

The trick was, of course, *don't make them think the queen is threatened.*

A kitten and an ice queen. With boxing gloves. Well, he'd known this would be complicated. He was really good at complicated.

He grinned. To be honest, he kind of assumed he was really good at everything, except losing.

"What's so funny?" Anne asked, her eyes narrowing a little.

"Me." He pushed some bubbles her way, let her feel clothed. Leaning back against the edge of the tub, he relaxed, deliberately not moving in on her. "Don't worry about the barbecue. They're probably over there debating the best way to ruin the ketchup now. And Dom and Luc don't really drink, but once the rest of them get started, they'll be there until six in the morning. Do you know the damn country even has a term for staying up until six in the morning drinking? Cade told me. They call it *refaire le monde.* Remaking the world." He rolled his eyes. "I mean, when I remake the world, the world can actually tell."

Anne laughed again, spontaneously, like sunlight flashing across...well, some very slushy ice at this point.

Must be disconcerting, to feel yourself getting so slushy. He didn't have that problem. He felt stronger and more intent every second.

He stretched his arm around the curve of the great, round tub and just casually, his arm relaxed against the edge, took her hand. He'd positioned himself so that was all they could reach—each other's hands, stretched out along the edge of the tub.

He took hers easily, playing with it idly, not holding on or trapping or possessing. Just stroking his thumb over her fingers, running it up between each one. Hell, he'd love a hand rub. Just giving her one made him think about how good it would feel to get one back.

She watched their hands with a very curious look on her face.

"How you feeling?" he asked, and then kicked himself. Christ, what kind of question was that? She might *tell* him.

But Anne, of course, gave him an appalled look.

That made him grin a little, but it also switched his mood around abruptly. Now he was a little pissed off that she *wouldn't* tell him. Which just proved that a man was an idiot to ask a question like that. Nothing good could come of it.

"Sore," she said crisply. "I mentioned."

He narrowed his eyes at her. "Are we going to do this the hard way?"

Her chin lifted a little, a gleam coming back into those moss-and-honey eyes. That brilliant pleasure in a challenge, instead of that shyness. "Possibly, Mack."

"Anne Lindsey Winters." He leaned forward in the bath and pointed one blunt finger at her. "We're sleeping in the same bed tonight. Don't you even *think* about using me and dumping me. Shit, I'm not that kind of man."

She bit back a grin—*another* one, hell, he was going to run out of fingers and toes to count them on soon. He started to settle back against the side smugly and then leaned straight back toward her, that dominating finger still bossing. "And another thing: I like to cuddle on the couch and watch inane movies that show no conception of the way the real world works, once in a while. *Bourne. Star Wars.* Not those new dipshit *Star Wars.* And I'm not putting up with any of that squirming away, putting pillows between us shit, or whatever you might be imagining."

She stared at him, that gold in her eyes like that early, early dawn sky, as light started to fill it. Little squeezing things were happening at the corners of her mouth that might be amusement or might be something more complex. "What if I like thoughtful, emotional dramas?"

Appalled, Mack sat all the way back, with a swoosh of water around the movement that lapped bubbles at her breasts. Which was about the coolest thing in the world, to be able to enjoy that view. "Since *when*? Are you kidding me?"

She raised her eyebrows just barely and gave a minute, haughty shrug of her bare shoulders. Again, the bubbles caressed the movement. Damn, but he liked that view. That vulnerability of only water and bubbles and her own haughtiness as a shield.

"Well, look," he decided. "We don't want to make Dad feel left out. We each get a turn picking one." If his dad even stuck around here for any time, given his fondness for following the girls to Paris. If he *was* around, Jack Corey wasn't going to be picking thoughtful, emotional dramas either, unless he did it just to torment his son. Mack could probably grind his teeth and endure one emotional drama every third movie night. It wouldn't be the first time he'd had to tolerate someone's movie choices, given that he'd raised two girls.

Although, to be honest, he'd infinitely prefer watching the Disney movies he'd had to endure with his girls over thoughtful, emotional dramas. Except *The Little Mermaid,* Jesus. The girls had had the damn thing memorized and would enact it throughout the house. And what the hell kind of role model was that, a girl who dumped her powerful dad to run off with some dipshit with black hair who couldn't even tell the difference between a real girl and a fake one? And signing contracts like that without even reading the fine print. Christ.

If Pixar and Blue Sky hadn't started coming out with movies like *Shrek* and *Ice Age,* he might have been warped for life.

"Mack," Anne said pityingly. "Thoughtful, emotional dramas? Seriously? You bought that?"

"Oh, thank God." Mack slumped deeper in the water in relief.

Anne burst out laughing. Just—laughter. Merry and free and—it was like being flooded with sunlight. That moment when the sun leaped over the ocean and blinded you until you wanted to open your arms to embrace its light but it was too much and it drove your eyes closed.

Hell. He ducked under the water, soaking his head a second, and peeked back up, just his eyes above the water, feeling like a damn frog.

Her eyes were tolerant, her chin superior—and she splashed him.

So he just ducked his head back under and twisted under water, sliding up past her breasts, to lift all the bubbles with his head and brace his arms over her. "Hey." He grinned down at her.

She scooped something off the top of his head without touching him and showed him the handful of bubbles. "You look ridiculous."

"You don't. You look fantastic." He kissed her. "Hell, you're hot." He nuzzled into the curve of her throat, because damn but he loved the pride in her shoulders, the line of her neck.

She traced over the muscles of his shoulder with one finger, down to his chest, and he liked the touch so damn much. It made his chest swell with happiness. Made him feel anything was possible. "You're mildly warm yourself," she said.

He laughed. "Flattery like that will get you absolutely nowhere." He kissed her again. She just—let him. Her mouth relaxing and responding. "I need more incentive. I think it's supposed to be, 'You are one sex god of a man, you. Take me now.'"

"Oh, I get to say *take* this time?" She arched an eyebrow.

He brought his lips to her ear. "It's not my *favorite* word in your mouth."

She thumped his shoulder, but not hard enough to sting.

He grinned into her shoulder and nipped it lightly. He felt like some great cat or something—just ridiculously, gloriously golden and happy. "Yeah, I'll get you to say it again. I've got *ideas.*"

She gave her elegant approximation of a snort. "I might have to start coming up with some of my own."

He reared back. "You don't already have some?" That was just rude. All the time they'd been walking on the beach together.

She gave him a Sphinx-like smile.

"If you do," Mack threatened, "I'm going to get those out of you, too. Just you wait."

She kept her smugly enigmatic Sphinx smile for a moment, but then it faded, and she rubbed that finger that had been on his chest against the edge of the tub. "Mack. About this sleeping together thing."

He narrowed his eyes and tightened the muscles in his arms on either side of her.

"I don't know how to *do* that."

"Well, hell, Anne, you think I remember? But I have a king size bed, so how about we each start out clinging to an edge, with pillows stacked between us, and just see what happens?"

"How about we *date* a while?"

He scowled, his whole body tensing. "Anne. Jesus."

"*I'm not good at this.*"

"Oh, fine. Shit." He shoved back across to the other side of the great round tub, folding his arms over his chest, sulking.

Not that he sulked or anything. He was head of one of the major corporations of the world. He had two grown daughters. Whom he'd taught not to sulk.

Anne folded her own arms over the breasts revealed by his displacement of bubbles and lifted her chin.

"Fine. We'll date. *This is the most ridiculous thing I've ever heard, Anne. We've been dating for a decade.* But we'll do it. I have a barbecue this afternoon. Informal. Wear whatever. It's just a chance for you to meet the family."

She rolled her eyes. "Now *you're* being ridiculous."

"You started it." Okay, maybe he might be capable of sulking a little. "And I'll take you out to breakfast tomorrow. After our walk." That walk was sacred. Plus, he'd need it, after seeing Jaime off for her honeymoon.

"I usually eat it in my breakfast room. I like the view of the sea."

"Perfect." His grin came back. Breakfast with Anne, looking out over the sea. Walks together, breakfast together, dinner…That transition to actually sleeping in the same bed was going to come a lot more naturally than she thought.

Personally—he grinned—he planned on going out like a *light* the next time they had sex, and being impossible to wake up.

Chapter 11

Anne's whole world had just done this stomach-lurching somersault and started rolling the opposite direction around the sun. She couldn't quite adjust. It was so different. She kept mistaking sunsets for sunrises.

And, seriously, Mack was just *bossy* about affection. He reached out when she tried to walk past him at the barbecue and looped her into his side, without ever breaking the rhythm of his argument with Sylvain about the value of producing a chocolate all could enjoy as opposed to a luxury item reserved for an elite. Granted, he could probably have that argument in his sleep by now, but still.

Cade dropped her burger on her toes.

He came up behind Anne while she was talking to Jaime about their honeymoon plans and planted a kiss right on the nape of her neck. Jaime broke into a delighted grin. Mack's kiss, meanwhile, shivered right down Anne's spine, over the curve of her butt, up through her sex, and might still have had enough shiver in it to curl her toes, too. That felt so...nice. *Kiss me again.*

He didn't, but he draped a hand over the back of her neck and rubbed lazily while he joined the conversation, that warm hand *heavenly*. She thought she might arch and purr like a cat. She thought she might turn into him, right there in front of his daughters and her son, and press her head to his shoulder.

"You're right," she overheard Jaime whisper a little while later to Dom. "They *weren't* together before. I wonder what changed?"

Big, bad Dom looked down at his new wife with the profoundest, most affectionate amusement, his hand lifting to curl over *her* nape and rub it lazily.

"Oh," Jaime said, and flushed. "Well, I wonder why now."

"They've both been shaken up," Dom said. "Prison for her, and you know that drove *him* out of his mind, and now his youngest daughter getting married—*merde,* it's got to be a lonely feeling for him, all of you moving to Paris. Maybe it all just helped shake some things out into the open."

Jaime's face screwed up. "She's a replacement for *us?*"

Dom's strong black eyebrows rose. "I thought you said they'd been best friends for most of your life."

Jaime nodded.

"Then she's not a replacement for anyone at all. She's herself."

Jaime rested a hand on his chest and smiled up at him. "How did you get so smart?"

Dom pulled her in closer to him and bent his head to her. "I read a lot of poetry," he said wryly.

Anne moved away, before she could eavesdrop herself into feeling even rawer.

Or...more solid?

She was herself.

That was incontrovertibly true.

She still even *felt* like herself. Just...warmed all through.

Not lonely.

And Mack—she looked across the garden at him, where he had gotten distracted by Sylvain again, because apparently Sylvain had had the nerve to flip one of the burgers while Mack's back was turned. Her shoulders relaxed just at the sight of him. The thought of him being able to reach casually out to her and wrap her up against him made her feel so *secure.*

As if she could do the same to him.

Until at some point, he stood with his hands in his pockets, talking to Summer, nodding seriously. He always did that, with Summer—tamed his hands a bit. Was careful not to impose himself on her, careful to show her respect and seriousness. Anne overheard the word *satellite*, and Mack nodded again, so determined to be a surrogate dad to Summer he'd probably buy her one— but only if she made a reasoned, convincing argument first. *I really love that man*, she thought, and it washed over her, the first time she had ever let her brain think it out loud.

But she'd loved him when he stood grim-faced in the courtroom, his fists clenched, barely able to restrain himself from leaping at her prosecution.

She'd loved him when he ripped chunks of the beach up and threw them into the waves, wracked with grief and rage for his daughter.

She'd loved him even when Julie died. This careful love she kept to herself, not this thing that kept her awake at night wishing for him or anything, just this secret, tender awe at the man handling that grief, struggling to be a good dad to his daughters.

She hadn't wanted to think about it. She hadn't wanted to say it in her head. But now that she thought about it, she realized it had always been true.

She slipped her own hands in her pockets and drifted up to him, not too different, really, from falling into step with him on the beach. His face lit—just lit, that radical change that had occurred in his happiness beaming out of him—and he wrapped an arm around her shoulders immediately. Anchoring her to his side. Affirming his claim.

Mine. She's mine. I, Mack Corey, own the world.

But she was Anne Winters. And she wasn't about to be *owned*. So she slipped one of her hands out of her pocket and slid it into the back pocket of his jeans. *Mine.* And she squeezed his ass, just a little.

He grinned as if she'd just put the Eiffel Tower on his birthday cake and lit it for him to blow out.

Mack Corey.

She shook her head a little bit, and when he glanced down at her, she smiled up at him.

"I'll do it," Mack told Summer. "You should have asked me in the first place. Shit, Summer." Even as he spoke, his attention completely on Summer, his thumb rubbed over the curve of Anne's shoulder, savoring it.

Summer shrugged in that sliding silk way she had and looked away, with that vague smile.

"You should have," Mack repeated more firmly. "Damn it, Summer. Julie must have told you a hundred times you could come to us whenever you needed."

Summer blinked. Anne saw her swallow hard, and those beautiful, ever-photographed blue eyes of hers shimmered suddenly with tears. Anne never let others see her tears, but she knew *exactly* where Summer's came from: just to have that strong, firm offer of human caring, of help. Of someone willing to be there when you needed him.

Over by Sylvain and Dom, Luc turned his head suddenly and his black gaze zeroed in on them, intent enough to cut. "I...she die—she d—she wasn't there anymore," Summer said softly.

Mack gave Anne a helpless look. "I'm sorry. We were such a mess after that, that I—that you—I'm sorry. But you still—" Then he conquered the helplessness—this man *always* conquered his helplessness—and spoke firmly. "I mean, I know Sam's your dad, Summer, and I can't do anything about that. But come to me if you need something. Don't go to him."

Summer blinked rapidly, and Anne bit the inside of her lip. That was a raw thing, to know your own dad was crappier than your cousins'. It was raw like having this hole in you that would never be filled with a baby, while some luminous, gorgeous blonde stood in front of you with a hand possessively caressing her rounded belly.

Neither Anne nor her daughter-in-law were likely to have more kids, any more than Summer was going to have her childhood transformed into one with loving parents. Sometimes you just had to deal with the cards life dealt you. Sam Corey, Summer's father, might be one of the wealthiest investors in the world, but he'd made a raw mess of his daughter.

Anne turned her head suddenly to find Kurt. Had she? Made a mess of her son? But Kurt and Kai were standing with the macaron chef, Philippe, and his wife Magalie. Kai was laughing, looking like her old self, and Kurt had a deep relaxation in his body. This profound ease of a man who had learned to wallow in every moment of happiness his life could hold. Anne didn't know if she could take any credit for it, but Kurt was happy.

Luc appeared by Summer's side, slipped his hand into her hair to rub it, and then let his hand slide down to her shoulder, massaging it almost exactly the way Mack was rubbing Anne's.

Summer took a long, slow breath and nodded once deliberately, that threat of tears fading. Her whole being strengthened, with that hand on her neck, infused with this quiet, intense happiness. "Thank you," she told Mack.

"Any time," Mack answered firmly, looking her in the eye.

Another little shimmer in Summer's eyes, that look of someone touched straight to the heart by kindness. She nodded and gave Mack a smile that was a little shy, as she turned to Luc. Luc, just before he drew her away, reached out and shook Mack's hand. Just this one firm clasp before he returned that hand to its pocket and headed off with her.

"He calls me *Monsieur*," Mack said finally to Anne, after the other couple had gone toward the boardwalk across the dunes. "Do you think I'll ever break him of that habit?"

"It's a high compliment," a sandy, sun-warmed voice mentioned from the other side of Mack. That blond surfer chef, Patrick, the only one with whom she had managed to get along, when they had invaded her kitchens the day before the wedding. He had a suppleness to him that was entirely deceptive. He winked at a woman, and it was about half an hour later before she realized that she had, indeed, gotten exactly what she wanted but that was only because her wants had somehow transformed into his. Patrick's fiancée was with him, tucked under his arm. Anne had liked her, too. Quiet and intense and perfectionist. And capable of letting Anne decide what happened in her own kitchens. "I mean, we're talking about a man who thinks *he's* God, you know. And he respects you."

"Then what the hell is wrong with my sons-in-law?" Mack demanded, rather than have to show how that touched him. "*They* don't respect me."

"Sure they do." Patrick gave him that lazy, charming grin. "That's why they fight it so hard."

Mack said nothing. But his lips curved just a little, in this repressed, intense satisfaction.

Patrick winked, tugged a lock of Sarah's black hair, and strolled off with her toward a hammock set up between the pool and the dunes.

"He's right about that," Anne said. "They can kind of cut their teeth on you, you know. Two strong-willed men who aren't used to an older man who has even more experience at strength than they do. They like it. Well, Dom might still feel a bit threatened. But that's not bad for him, you know, to get used to a strong older man who's never going to misuse his power. It might even help him learn how to be a man like that himself—and he might even know that and be hungry for it, deep down. You give them both someone to strengthen themselves against."

Mack turned toward her, realization softening his gaze and lighting it. He lifted his hand to touch the feathered edge of her hair. "Like you do for me."

O—

Oh.

Oh, the *power* of that. The way it spread out from her middle in this shock wave of sweetness.

It almost made her eyes want to shimmer like Summer's.

"It's, ah—it's mutual." She rested her hand on his chest. She did want this intimacy, she did. It was just so scary, so unfamiliar. But the feel of his warm body under her hand made her draw a breath of pleasure. *He* drew one, too, the light brightening in his eyes.

"You're a big man," she said quietly, looking up at him.

His eyes crinkled a little, in confused pleasure. "Both my sons-in-law are taller than I am."

"No, I mean—you. You're a big man."

His expression got all funny. He looked almost *flustered*. Mack Corey. Was that *color* on his cheekbones?

"This isn't the first time I've ever told you something like this," she mentioned curiously. On those beach walks, it wasn't as if they didn't talk about things that were meaningful.

"It...goes deeper." His hand slid to cover hers on his chest. "When you've got your hand right here." He pressed it more firmly, until she could feel the thump of his heart.

"Yes," she agreed low. "Everything's a lot more vulnerable that way."

He let his other hand drop down to her shoulder to tug her toward him. "I like it. But it's hard, as you said." His strong fingers rubbed her shoulder. "Maybe harder on you?"

She raised her eyebrows, denying she could be weaker in any way.

"Because the people who got deep inside here," he pressed her hand harder to his heart, "and left me did it because they grew up, because they were supposed to do that and I was supposed to give them wings to do it. Or they did it because they couldn't help it." Julie, of course. "But that person who got deep inside you and let you down—he just failed you. No excuses."

"I might have been the excuse," Anne managed, half-wryly. She touched her belly, a gesture she had thought abandoned so long ago. "There were these other little people, deep inside me, that *I* let down, maybe, only it felt more complicated than that. Like maybe they abandoned me despite everything I could do. And I reacted to it so badly that...you can't really blame Clark."

Although she had, and still did. And watching her son with Kai, she blamed Clark again. *You could have been my strength. The only time in my life I ever needed someone besides myself to be strong.*

Unless you counted that slow, steady, constant support of those walks on the beach. Unless you counted a man fighting vicious and enraged, with every dirty trick he had in the book, against the judicial system, and then gripping your hands when everything failed you, willing you your own strength, feeding it: *You can survive this. You're Anne Winters. You can do anything.*

"To be honest, Anne, I think I could walk on Clark and never even notice. I don't know if you call that blame exactly, but he sure as hell didn't deserve *you*."

"That's what I decided, too," Anne allowed.

Mack smiled a little, and his hand curved around her nape, rubbing it. "But that doesn't mean *no* man is capable of deserving you." He angled his head and considered. "Or maybe no man is, but I'm grabbing you, just the same."

She couldn't stop herself from smiling, almost shiveringly flattered, like a young girl trying to handle a compliment.

A young girl. Her. She felt like one, though. Vulnerable. New.

I'm scared of this much happiness. It swelled all around her, vast, reaching out to every horizon. She had never known happiness could be so big.

Or if she had, it had been so long ago, in that innocent, buoyant optimism with which she had fallen in love with Clark, gotten married, started her business.

She'd been happy then, and later had just assumed that happiness was like some kind of balloon, based on innocence, lightness, and helium, and that the first encounter with reality popped it. She hadn't known that happiness, when it had a lot of experience at life behind it and still managed to grow, could be *bigger.*

Stronger.

Something *sturdy.*

She closed her eyes, against the sun of him, letting him glow against her eyelids, warming her face. Tension melted out of her. So strange. She hadn't known she was tense.

Did she not even know how her body felt relaxed?

He tugged her around the corner of the house, until they were out of sight of the others, and then just tugged her again, into his arms, snuggling her in. God, he was good at that. The snuggle. Did it come from having two girls to raise? If she'd had a daughter, would she have been good at it? Was it her fault Kurt had lost the taste for cuddles by the time he was seven?

"Shh," he murmured, as if she'd argued, when she hadn't said a word. His hand rubbed her nape, dissolving her body more into him. More resistance melted out of her that she hadn't even known her muscles were making, her body hot and cherished.

She kept her eyes closed. *I think I'll just melt here.* It sounded like such a good way to go.

He leaned back against the wall of the house so that he could angle more of her weight onto him. Mmm. Maybe she would just go to sleep.

"I'm surprised I found a private spot free." Mack's grumble was deep but barely spoken aloud, as if he was just providing a little brown noise for her. "I can barely turn a corner without coming across someone making out."

It was true that happiness packed this house and its grounds right now. Anne's face softened into a smile. That was what she'd always wanted the spaces she designed to hold.

"Usually some idiot with one of my daughters."

Her smile deepened. Her hand slipped, all unplanned, around his waist and rubbed his ribs a little. "You like them."

A rumbling protest under her ear.

Mmm, the vibration. She wanted to make him rumble again. But words took effort, pulling her away from this feeling.

"Anne," he murmured, wondering. His hand kept petting her nape, a thumb stroking up over the base of her skull. "This is so nice." He sounded as if he couldn't believe in it, how nice it was.

Neither could she. And yet it felt so entirely—credible. Real.

"You think we could just stretch out in one of the hammocks?" he asked. Cautiously. Mack Corey, cautious. *Because she could say no.* "I know we're the hosts, but...that way I wouldn't have to see when they make a macaron burger, or whatever they're likely to do next. Let the kids take charge. That's what I trained them to be able to do."

A hammock sounded nice.

Really nice.

Really, incredibly nice.

She turned her head. Patrick and his fiancée Sarah lay in one, Patrick smiling up at the sycamore tree above him, one hand behind his head, the other lazily tracing Sarah's spine.

An empty one, over there, didn't exactly hide them from any curious younger generation, but it had a gentle sense of seclusion. She always thought about things like that when she was designing gardens: what would be comfortable, what would be inviting.

And it was inviting.

She nodded against Mack's chest.

His hand tightened just a second on her nape. "Hey, really?"

Before she could answer, he was already seizing the opportunity, heading them toward the hammock.

When he settled back into it and pulled her in after him, his grin was a sunburst inside her. All that happiness just to be with her.

Anne had no idea how to share a hammock, especially in a skirt. Mack took up a heck of a lot of space, and his weight pulled the canvas all toward him, so that she was the one who had to tumble into him. It wasn't such a bad warmth and strength to be tumbled into, though.

Actually, it felt pretty damn good.

She shifted onto her back so that she could gaze at their hammock's sycamore tree, with a smile that was probably pretty close to Patrick's. Relaxed. Blissful. The sycamore's mottled gray-green bark showed all its struggles to grow—the stretches and the splits, the chunky, rippled way it tried to fill in for the growth of the trunk. It had a hard time growing bigger than itself, the sycamore. And yet it kept on doing it just the same.

Unexpectedly, her mind flashed back to prison, the little things she'd learned from it. Like how much *life* she had, to savor. How *big* the world was, outside an eight by six cube. And, no matter how iconic your look was, how you should always let a woman dreaming of freedom cut your hair.

That even dreams were a privilege. It had driven her completely mad, the need to get permission for the haircut. But she had learned some things.

She'd learned she acted almost the same way in prison as she did everywhere else. Closed off. Walls up. Ready to fight anyone who got too close back from her.

Some people stayed in the eight by six cubes. They got themselves sent back when they were released, because within that routine, that space, they felt safer.

She didn't have to be that way.

Mack shifted onto his side, head propped on one hand. Of course that messed up her position—big, dominant, bossy man, even when he didn't realize it— and she shifted sideways, too, restoring her comfort. Now her back nestled against his chest. He rubbed a slow path down her arm. "You're so hot." The low rumble of compliment could have been a code for three other words, the way he said it. "Have I mentioned how sexy you are?" His big hand rubbed over her wrist, linked fingers with hers, this tender, stroking motion of that heat and tough palm that sent tremors of pleasure all through her.

She smiled. At fifty-three, it was pretty damn good to be sexy.

"Thanks for the fight," she murmured.

Mack didn't answer for a moment, and she twisted back around enough to catch the guilty twist to his lips. "Anne. Half my fantasies for making love to you involved me *making* you *like it*. Taking your *no* and *conquering* it. I'd *kill* any man who had those fantasies about my daughters. Except then you *told* me to and—Christ, that was hot."

Against her bottom, she could feel him growing aroused again just at the memory. It made her bottom feel—naughty. Like it wanted to wiggle a tiny bit and gloat over his helpless position to do anything about it out in public in this hammock.

She maybe didn't wiggle it, exactly, but she shifted position carefully to make herself comfortable. Naturally her butt had to shift a little back and forth for that, too.

A deep sound of approval vibrated into her spine from his chest.

Her smile felt secret and smug. "Well. You know how much I love a good fight," she said to the hammock fabric.

Mack's laughter was a delicious texture against her back. "I might have a tiny taste for battle, too."

Her smile deepened. She might even have let her gluteus maximus squeeze a little bit against a certain hardness. "Maybe we're made for each other."

His fingers flexed against hers, his thumb rubbing along the side of her palm. His breath brushed across her temple. "You're a self-made woman, Anne."

Yes.

"And not to discount my father's achievements before I took over the company, but I'm pretty much a self-made man."

Yes. He'd started on the shoulders of giants, as it were, with his family's multimillion-dollar company, but he was the one who had forged it into the multibillion-dollar global power it was today.

"So we made ourselves for each other?" Mack asked.

Anne found herself smiling foolishly, half her smile pressed into the hammock, too happy even to turn around.

Mack lifted her hand, fingers still linked, his hand still covering the back of hers, and kissed the bend of her wrist. "Been wanting to do that," he murmured, and tucked both their hands back against her belly, embracing her.

His head sank onto the hammock. His body eased around hers, strength relaxing. "This is really nice, Anne," he sighed.

Sun and shadow blurred against her eyelids as she fell asleep.

Chapter 12

Mack woke her involuntarily, trying to slip out of the hammock. "Sorry." He laid his palm over her forehead and stroked it down over her eyes, closing them. His thumb grazed over her temple, and her eyelashes kept trying to press back open against his hand. Not really fighting the gesture, just wanting to see this strong, tough hand that had come into her world and touched her with so much warmth and gentleness. "Go back to sleep."

Of course, she couldn't go back to sleep—it was an astonishing break from habit that she had taken a nap at all—but she didn't try to sit up. Curled onto her side, she gazed at nothing really, dreams in the air, perhaps, or the astonishing dream-like shape that reality had taken.

Mack's face appeared in front of hers as he crouched down to bring himself to eye level. His grin flashed. "Notice how easy that was?"

She narrowed her eyes at him, but a smile tried to fight its way up around the corners of her lips. "Sleeping?"

"Sleeping with me." He ran a thumb over her lips and pressed it into the lower one like a kiss, then he was up and moving away.

"I was tired!" Anne called after him.

He stuck his hand behind his back and shot her a bird.

She burst out laughing. And watched *his* ass as he walked away from her, apparently to resolve something that needed the host's input. Possibly Sylvain might have raised an eyebrow at the selection of mustard.

Watching his butt made her hands tickle. Like she wanted to be the kind of person who could reach right out and give that butt a pretend smack when he was teasing her.

And maybe she could.

He turned, just before he rounded the corner of the house, and gave her a smug smile over his shoulder, making a gloating show of licking his finger and scoring a point for himself in the air, and she laughed so hard, she had to sit up in the hammock and bury her head in her hands. The laughter swelled out of her like bottled up champagne—shaken up, cork popped off, fizzing out.

I love that man. It was getting easier to think. Loved him so much it made her helpless with delight, and she hated helplessness. She did.

But just—right at that moment, being helpless with *delight* didn't seem that bad.

She finally looked up, spotting Kurt.

He was standing at some distance, near the boardwalk over the dunes, as if he'd caught sight of her on his way back from the beach. His face, as their eyes met, slowly split into the most delighted beam. Just boyishly *thrilled*, as if he was ten years old again and she was doing the one cool mom act she had, taking him on all the biggest roller coasters with nerves of steel.

He was that happy...to see *her* happy?

She got up suddenly and hurried across the grass to him, as close to running as that time she'd just spotted him in the airport after he returned from his first two-week summer visit with his father. She'd tried to control herself, tried not to show how ragged his absence had made her feel. Maybe she should have just broken out and run.

His happiness got overtaken by confusion, even some wariness, as she stopped right in front of him. Her beautiful, hazel-eyed son.

She threw her arms around him suddenly and hugged him as tightly as she could. "I love you *so much*," she told him fiercely. His heart thumped hard under her ear against his chest. She pulled back a little, still holding on. "Have I told you that enough?"

He searched her face cautiously. "Not—not very often, Mom."

Wait, what? Didn't he *know*? She thrust her hands up into his hair, holding his face between her palms, all that love and happiness that had been surging up in her suddenly finding a place where it absolutely needed to go. "You're the best thing that ever happened to me. The very best thing."

His breath caught. Those beautiful, careful, sensitive eyes of his widened, and then he hit something, something painful, in his head, and his lips twisted a little. "Even if you wanted better?"

It shook her so hard it hurt. She stared at him. "I never—there isn't *better*."

"Mom." He turned his head away, his mouth tightening.

"Kurt." She shook his head a little between her hands. Pain stole her breath. How could he possibly, possibly think that?

"Mom." His expression tightened, as he tried not to speak. And yet the words slipped out anyway: "I know what happened when you couldn't have another child after me. I was there, all right? Just—" He shook his head and angled his face farther away.

She gasped. The intense and utter cruelty of so many years of love—failed. Misunderstood. Not expressed enough or right. "Kurt. It wasn't...I was so happy with you. I knew I needed...more. It was too intense, it was too scary, how much I loved you, how much every single thing about me depended on you. I— I wanted three or four of you. I wanted *spares*. I wanted to see what you would be like if you were a girl, or if you were a wild rebel, or all the variations of you that there could possibly be. I don't—I wanted more kids because I loved so much the one I *already had*."

Kurt stood very still, his breath this shallow, tight thing that she recognized so much from when he was a little boy struggling with emotion, trying to be a big boy, because his idiot dad told him big boys didn't cry. Fuck Clark, anyway. Mack Corey cried. And you didn't get much bigger than that.

Sometimes you cried because there was too much of you to hold in a human body. Laughter, joy, rage, pain, you had to let some of it out.

"Mom." His eyes were red, and he was doing that pinching movement of his nose that meant he was fighting with all his might the sting in it.

She wrapped her arms around him and hugged him hard again. Just hugged him as if she could turn back time to when he was still a little boy who loved cuddles and if she hugged him hard enough she would never, ever have to let him go.

Never once, ever, be too busy or too stressed with a growing business or her failing marriage or her post-miscarriage depression and give him just a short, quick hug and tell him to go play.

"Kurt." She shook her head helplessly. "Every beautiful moment in my life came from you."

"Mom." His eyes were definitely dampening now, and his mouth crooked all funny, embarrassed and touched. "You know that can't possibly be true."

"You don't—" *know anything about being a parent,* she had started to say and caught herself just in time. How easily a person could cause careless, cruel wounds, without ever even realizing it. "—understand. From the moment you were born, you just...held my heart."

From the flicker in his eyes, Kurt realized, at least partially, what she had avoided saying. Or else he was thinking about how some little kid might never hold his heart.

His head turned. He was looking for his wife. For Kai, who might have torn his heart into pieces, but who still held all those pieces in her hand. Anne found herself

146

wanting to glance around for Mack. For that strong, sure hand to help hold *her* heart. To not leave all of her pieces in the hands of a son who clearly needed both hands these days just to hold his wife's.

They leave you. It sighed through her like waves on a beach.

And, that vital, utterly strong voice: *Yeah, I don't do that leaving shit.*

She tightened her arms around her son.

"Thank you, Mom," Kurt said very softly, and bent and kissed the top of her head. He stood for a moment, his hands resting awkwardly on her shoulders, and then, as she kept hugging him, slipped his arms around her and gave her a sudden, fierce squeeze back. "*Thank you.*"

She let him go, reluctantly, and they both took a deep breath. He gave her a shaky, wondering, hopeful smile, and then walked quickly back toward the beach. She watched him stop at the railing out where the benches were. He stood there a while, and then headed out onto the beach. Kai came out of the house in time to spot him, waved at Anne, and headed after him.

So he would be all right. Kai would hold his hand, and they would walk on the beach, and maybe he would tell her all the things wrong with his relationship with his mother, all the things Anne had screwed up.

Or maybe they wouldn't talk about her at all.

Maybe that might even be for a good reason, because Kurt was holding this moment just now in his own heart.

She wanted Mack, Anne thought.

And her heart eased. Because, here was the wonderful thing—she could have him. He said so. She didn't even have to wait until their beach walk in the morning.

***

It was midnight, though, before they could escape. Funny, no matter how old your kids got, you wanted to keep in the vicinity, just in case they ever called, "Mommy!" again.

A breeze came off the water, autumn thinking about its approach run. Mack's mouth was drooping, and he didn't talk. Jaime and Dom were heading off first thing in the morning for their honeymoon in Papua New Guinea, and Cade would be flying back to Paris with all those chefs who couldn't take any more time off. Mack's nest was officially, entirely empty.

"At least you did a good job with them," Anne said finally. That thing she'd had on her heart all day, waiting for this walk with him. "I was a crappy mom to Kurt, I guess."

Mack's head was still bent, inspecting the midnight beach far too diligently for shells, but he slid her a glance. "It shows," he said dryly. "Successful lawyer, happily married, able to surmount an incredible hurdle and still hold his marriage together."

Well...yes, but Kurt might be managing that *despite* her. "He's taking a year off as a lawyer to travel around the world," Anne managed, finally. Granted, that was a little lame, as an argument to defend her right to feel terrible about herself. Talk to Mack for any length about your problems and pretty soon you couldn't find a single weak spot in yourself anymore. He'd turn them all into strengths.

Mack grunted and shrugged those broad shoulders. "Look at Cade and Jaime. You think they're putting career first? But then again—" He took a deep breath, gazed out across the moon-glazed water, and heaved a sigh. "Well, there's probably not much point them putting making money as a top priority, is there? I mean, you and I have kind of got that covered for them. They're just...re-evaluating our priorities. Putting their family first. But they can only do that because *we* put them first—gave them as much power and money as we could." And that bitter, savage twist to his lips that meant, *Much good it did them.* That meant he was thinking of Jaime...and maybe of Anne, too, and her battle against the Justice Department.

Her gaze slid down to his hand in his pocket. They did that so automatically, after so many years—thrust their hands in their pockets to keep from touching each other while they walked side by side. If he thought about it, she was pretty sure Mack would reach out and grab her hand now in that tight, bossy grip that dared her hand to argue.

But he hadn't thought about it. The habit was ingrained in him so deeply that he couldn't automatically reach for her hand, when he needed it.

Anne took a deep breath and slid her hand in between his pants and his wrist, nudging her fingers a tiny bit toward the palm hidden in his pocket.

His face brightened up *so much.* "Hey." His hand slid instantly out of his pocket to take hers, firm and strong. "Hey," he said again, softly, as if he'd just found a baby unicorn on the beach and didn't want to scare it into the water.

She snuggled her hand a little in his, astonished by this whole sensation. Of being held, of being cherished. It scared the freaking hell out of her.

As if she could collapse on this beach and vomit at the thought of losing it, and she hadn't vomited loss and pain out in a long, long time. And sure as hell not in front of someone else.

"Fits pretty well, doesn't it?" Mack asked smugly, adjusting his grip around hers. "I'm good at this hand-holding business. Just ask Cade and Jaime."

"I'm not a small girl-child," Anne said ironically. And she didn't want to break his heart or anything, but his girls probably didn't even remember. She was pretty sure Kurt had forgotten all the times she'd held *his* hand crossing a street, just to make sure he was safe.

"I was good with Julie, too," Mack argued his corner automatically. As always. And then realized, his gaze sliding warily to hers. "That is—maybe I shouldn't—"

"I'm really not that insecure," Anne said very, very dryly.

Mack gave a shout of laughter. "No, by God, you aren't." He turned her into his arms abruptly. Damn, but he could take control of her body so easily. Only—he made it feel like dancing. She wanted him to dip her. She wanted to dance and be happy. She wanted to take a year off and travel around the world with him, like Kurt and Kai, and she'd been a compulsive workaholic all her life. She'd actually chosen to go to *prison*, instead of appeal, so she could get the whole damn trial thing out of the way in a more efficient six months and get back to concentrating on her work. "You sure as hell aren't," he whispered, his hand coming up to stroke so tenderly over the feathered edges of her hair.

Wonder washed through her. She couldn't help it— she rubbed her temple against his fingertips.

"You're so *pretty*," he said incredulously. "Oh, my God, you're pretty, in the moonlight, with your lashes lowering like that. *Shit*, Anne." His hand curved under her jaw, big and warm against her fine bones, and kept her face up so he could enjoy it. "It's like I've captured a star-queen."

She shivered so much with pleasure it was all she could do not to press against him for his solidity and warmth. "You don't mean an Ice Queen?" She tried to make that a mocking note in her voice and not a bitter one. All the time she had spent trying to make the world perfect for people, and all the hatred that had poured out on her when that trial started. So many people so happy to see her torn down. Maybe that was another reason she'd chosen not to appeal. Because, you know, fuck them.

"Funny thing about ice." His fingers shaped her head. "When light hits it, God, how it shines." His thumb ran over her lips, and she couldn't breathe. She wanted to do so many things—suck his thumb into her mouth, run into the cold ocean, stand still to savor this. Only she couldn't stand still—all of her felt as if it was sliding out of her body, into the sand, into his hands, running away from her.

"You make me feel all *liquid*," she said, frantic with helplessness.

"*Good*." He kissed her. This hot, sweet warmth rushing straight from his body into hers, melting her everywhere.

She kissed him back, clinging to his shirt with both hands, stretching the cotton into her fists' shape. Kissed and was kissed until she had to rest her head on his chest. "I don't think I know how to do this anymore," she whispered.

His hands rubbed down her back, kneading her body into his. His chest lifted and fell against her head and breasts. "It's not like riding a bicycle," he murmured, voice gone gravelly. "You have to learn it new, with each new person, if you want to do it right. You're the first you I've ever kissed."

She smiled a little into his chest. "We're like a snowflake." She could whisper that fancy into this moonlit, ocean-washed night. "No two pairs of lips meet the same."

"You're exactly right." Mack lifted her face to his again. "Anne." He parted her lips for him, found her tongue. "If you really were an icicle, I'd suck you all over until you melted to nothing in my mouth."

God. That was so sweet and so erotic both. Her hands climbed up around his neck, and she pressed herself into him, heat against heat.

"It's a good thing you're human instead." He scooped under her bottom, pulling her up until her pelvis fit with his. "So I can suck you all night and you'll still be left for me to suck on again tomorrow."

He dropped them down onto the sand suddenly, pulling her astride him and clamping his hands onto her thighs to hold her there as he kissed her more. His mouth by turns fierce and hungry and...sweet. Tender. Fierce again. And tender once more.

Her breath grew shallow, this tenderness undoing her. He found her collarbone and kissed and kissed across that sensitive skin to the hollow of her throat and then he dropped back, lying on the sand under her as she sat astride him. Her slim skirt rode too far up her thighs for this public space, and his jeans pressed too intimately into her thin panties. But she didn't move. "*Look* at you," he breathed. "With the moon and the sea behind you. God."

Her heart thumped so hard it felt—it felt like a heart. Like those fairytale hearts you read about, the ones that lodged in your throat, that hurt you, that tore out of your body and put themselves into someone else's hands. *Be gentle with my heart. No one else ever has been.*

She'd only ever really given it to Clark, Kurt, and her unborn babies before. Clark had been the wrong place to put it. And children didn't know how to be gentle with their parents' hearts.

"Look at you," she whispered. Stretched out on the sand for her. In her power and not humbled by it at all. "You're one confident man."

In the moonlight, his blue eyes looked as black and brilliant as the sea. Funny, how the light and darkness playing over the hard planes of his face didn't make him look a stranger at all. He still looked entirely hers.

"You know when I said I was a self-made man?" He lifted a hand from the sand to stroke from her shoulder to her wrist, leaving grains of sand on her skin. It was growing far too cool for the short sleeves she had worn during the heat of the day, and she shivered toward his warmth. "I made a mistake."

Her eyebrows went up. "You?"

"Yeah." His eyebrows drew together in bafflement, as he pulled her hand onto his chest, rubbing himself with her fingers. "I don't know how I could have made such a stupid mistake. I left out you."

Her heart caught. And then it just broke. Like an icicle shattered off a tree.

"I left out my daughters, and Julie, and my dad. And *you.* All the ways you've helped me grow and—be. Be strong. Be me. Be—big. And be okay. Be sane. Be, you know, the best me I could be."

That shattered spot where her heart had been filled up with liquid until it leaked into her lungs, making it too hard to breathe, and then it filled up her eyes. She was drowning under it, and she clutched her hands into the muscles of his chest for him to save her.

"Mack. Please. I don't think I can—" handle this. Be this real. Be this vulnerable.

He sat up again suddenly and wrapped his arms around her, so that she was astride his lap and pulled in tight against his chest.

And suddenly—she was still vulnerable. But she was vulnerable in such a protected spot. He had her covered.

"*I really love you,*" she whispered suddenly, fiercely, and then twisted her mouth into his shirt, trying, too late, to shut herself up.

His body jerked. "Hey. *Hey.*" He caught her chin, lifting her face from his shoulder. "You just—*said* that. I can't believe you *told* me that." His face filled with wonder and happiness.

She twisted her chin free from his hand and buried her face in him again. "Damn it, I'm so scared."

His arms tightened around her fiercely. "*Eight fucking days a month.*" The words ground out of him. "That's how often I could see you those six months in prison. That's how often I could check to see that you were okay. And the rest of the time, I could do *nothing.* I lost my wife fifteen years ago. Somebody beat the fucking crap out of my daughter. *You think I don't know how scary loving someone is?* I got nothing, Anne. But *you* can do this. You're *Anne Winters,* hell. Just tough it the fuck up."

She drew a shaky breath, and then another. And slowly, slowly, all that fear in her began to calm. Began to ease its way out of her muscles, slide off her into the strength of his hold, drain away from both of them into the sand. The hush of the ocean washed slowly over her mind. "You say *fuck* to me a lot," she murmured finally. Because saying inconsequentials made her feel more solid, more grounded in him. As if all of this could become her normal life.

"I'm trying to get you into the habit." He kissed somewhere near her ear. "You know how much I love it when you say it."

She pushed herself enough away from him to try to give him a wry, warning look.

"Aww, sweetheart." He ran his thumb down her cheek. "You really did turn liquid." He held up his wet finger to her. "And I was right. It shimmers in the moonlight."

She pushed at the tears on her other cheek. He caught her hand and forced it down, in that battle for dominance that sent a little jolt of eroticism right through her body. His teeth showed like a wolf threatening a challenger. "I thought I told you I needed more salt in my diet." But when his mouth touched her skin, it was just his lips, as he traced the path of her tears very gently, sucking with infinite tenderness little sips of her tears.

"Damn you, Mack." She started crying harder.

"They taste...precious. But I might be biased." He brought them both to their feet and then just lifted her into his arms.

"Mack." She was slightly horrified, and she was still struggling not to lose more tears. Except—she didn't mind giving him precious parts of herself. She just couldn't stand the weaknesses. Were her tears really precious? "You're going to ruin your back."

"You overestimate your weight. You always did tend to think your body was as big as your spirit." He headed toward her house.

"I can walk on my own two feet, you know." She shifted uncomfortably but didn't want to struggle more because she really was worried she would throw out his back.

"I do believe you've established that already, Anne. Guess what I don't seem to have proven to you yet? That when necessary, I can carry you."

"I can't carry you," she said stiffly. Physically, she was average height. But she had never liked admitting she was smaller than most men.

He gave her an incredulous look. "Jesus, Anne. You carried me for years after Julie died. Months after Jaime. Hell, part of you is still carrying me *right now*. You still don't quite understand how our architecture works, do you?"

"I've never been that good at couples."

His grin broke out. "You're such a damn liar. You've had my back for twenty years. You're just not good at admitting you need me at yours. You're kind of like a unilateral couple, that's your problem. We need to fix that."

They reached her boardwalk. Mack put her down only because her feet kept bumping into the railing.

Walking up the ramp with him just behind her was...erotic. Each footstep against the boards this thump of his approach. Each step she took an expression of her willingness for him to follow.

By the time she got to the end of it, the muscles of her bottom itched so much for touch that she wanted to knead her buns herself. She stopped suddenly on purpose, just so he would run into her and she could feel that jolt of contact through her body.

"I don't know whether it's the boxing or the yoga, but you have a really great ass, Anne," Mack murmured to the top of her head. "You know, in one of my fantasies, I smash you up against the shower wall, and I run my hands all over that butt, and oh, my God, the expression on your face when I do it—I think that one usually starts with me surprising you in the shower—but then, of course, I make you *like* it, until you're all moaning and slippery and—"

She licked her lips, heat curling and pooling into places she'd never even understood it could. Her *throat* felt flushed, as if she wanted to tilt her head back and bare it. And her *elbows* tickled, as if she needed to clamp them to her sides. She turned toward him, there in her fairytale garden.

He rested his hands on her hips and snugged them in close to him. "You know how I told you half my fantasies about you involve winning, breaking through, making you like it?"

She gave him a wry, challenging smile to cover how hard that made her heart beat.

"Half of them don't involve any of that at all."

A little jolt of confusion, her world scrambling to get ready for its next re-ordering.

"Some of them *you* come on to *me*. Because, you know, you can't resist me anymore. Or because you want to wield your power over *me*, break *me*. And God almighty, do I like it when you conquer me. And some of them are so gentle, I fall to sleep dreaming in the middle of them." He lifted that strong, tender hand to her hair as he seemed to like to do. Every time he traced the edge of her hair, the shape of her head, it felt as if he was trying to trace the shape of *her*. Of who she was. Carefully. As if that shape of her was a miracle. "I never had one that took place in a hammock before today," he murmured.

She glanced toward the nearest hammock in her yard.

Out under the stars like that, in the cool of a September evening by the sea? It sounded...beautiful.

"I'm not even sure it's possible to have sex in a hammock," Mack added.

Oh. Yeah, probably not.

He ran his hand up her back, that deep frisson of pleasure. "I bet you can make love in one, though. You can make love anywhere."

"In a crowded train?" Anne challenged immediately. She couldn't help herself. She *had* to challenge. When she felt vulnerable, it was so hard not to fight everyone back from her walls.

"Sure." He pulled her toward the hammock. "I'd put my hand on your knee, if we were sitting." He touched her knee. "Block the rest of the crowd from you if we're standing." He braced one arm against the tree behind her, holding her in against it with his body, as if it was a pole on a subway and a crowd was pressing into them. His scent touched her subtly: sun and sea and grilling. "Maybe touch your face while we ratchet along the tracks." He lifted his other hand in that gentle, *you-are-so-special-to-me* caress against the edge of her hair.

This whole new definition of *making love* snuck into her heart and filled it up. Oh. Was that her *heart* again? That thing that had been shattered and its hole filled with liquid? It felt different now. It felt beating, warm. Swollen, so that the wrong rough touch could pop it. "In the middle of a restaurant?" she tried, just to hear what he would say.

"Oh, that's easy. I'd look at you, across the table." He held her eyes, with a little smile. "I'd touch your hand." His fingers brushed across the back of her palm, and she felt...romantic. Courted. Loved. "I'd ask you what you think of the wine." He touched his thumb to her lower lip. "Because I'd want to know if your mouth was happy with me."

He did that already, whenever they were out to dinner. Nodded at the waiter to make sure she was served a taste, too, if the waiter was still clueless enough not to offer it automatically. Looked across the table, caught her eyes, maybe just raised his eyebrows to see what she thought. And she would tilt her head, considering, or just give a flicker of a smile and nod. Sometimes he would talk about it more, after the waiter left. *What do you think of the oak? Too much? Are you picking out that hint of blackberry and chocolate he was talking about? Because I'm picking up more on just, you know, wine.*

He'd been doing that for a decade.

"In a—in a hammock?" Her voice shushed itself out, yielding itself to softer, more delicate actions.

He pulled her down with him into the hammock, tucking her body up against his, back to his chest, just the way they had slept that afternoon when all the lingering wedding guests were around. "I guess we still need to figure out what works." He lifted a hand to her temple and drew his fingers slowly, slowly down the line of her body, around the curve of her ear, down her throat, over her shoulder, down her arm, slipping onto her thigh, following it to her knee before he ran out of arm reach. Pleasure ran through her in the path of his hand, this exquisite sense of being precious to someone.

"What do you think? Does that work, Anne?"

She might have made a sound. Her head bent forward into the canvas.

"What about this, sweetheart?" His blunt fingers rested at the base of her skull and then oh-so-gently caressed down the back of her neck, lingering at the nape. "Does that feel like making love, to you?"

She couldn't answer. How was she supposed to answer? He stole all words. And in their place he left the essence of—her. And, in his hands, *her* was a very precious thing.

His hand slipped over her collarbone, found the hollow of her throat, traced over the upper swell of her breasts. So strange to realize that this blunt, tough businessman, with his square hands and his impossibly intense need to dominate the world, had this much tenderness in him. She'd known he had that much *love—*

she'd seen it, with Julie, with his children—but it had never even occurred to her that he could be capable of such a delicate touch.

It turned her delicate, too. It made her feel like a snowflake resting on a human palm, struggling not to lose her shape.

And then the shape of her was gone. She was only water. And that, it turned out, was the essence of who she was. The rest of it—the snowflakes, the ice—were just ways she manifested herself, sometimes, to a cold world.

"What about this?" he whispered.

She twisted around to bury herself in him. "Mack." Her voice felt strangled and desperate. She kissed *his* collarbone, the hollow of his strong throat.

Pleasure rumbled through him. Why did pleasure always strengthen him while it weakened her?

He arched his throat to her willingly, showing how much he liked it, and so she kissed her way to his jaw. His afternoon shadow made her lips prickle, and she drew back a little to lick them.

He drew a breath. She had risen a little above him, and now he looked up at her face, his gaze focusing on her lips. Funny, even with the night and moonlight to hide lines, he still didn't look like the man she had met twenty years ago, when she bought the house next door. He'd already had a few lines at the corners of his eyes and a fair amount of gray hair back then, even though he'd only been thirty-three. But he'd been smoother, everywhere, more arrogance than substance. Now that arrogance had proven itself. It was arrogance like a rock, grown rugged with experience.

His voice had changed, too. That smooth, powerful voice he had had, that could control the meetings of the mighty—Julie's death had roughed it up. Anne's own throat tightened still in sympathy at the thought of the grief that had strained his throat so badly. Then more recently, Jaime. And her. His voice grown so raw and strained with fury during her trial that she'd half expected him to lose it entirely in some height of rage.

But it had kept going, that voice. That man. Roughed up, but determined.

"Kiss me," that voice whispered now.

She smiled, her hand tracing oh-so-gently over the face that bad-tempered time was starting to batter. What was he always telling her? "Mack. Shhh."

She kissed him.

The sweetest, truest kiss. It started out so gentle, but it grew, and then it grew, until it felt as endless as the waves of the sea. It even fell into the waves' rhythm— kiss and breath, kiss and breath, lips and tongue sliding against each other, in and out as if they were the edge of sea and land.

"Anne," he managed so much later she had no idea how many waves had hit that beach, "I think this hammock is driving me crazy."

He'd been in her bedroom before, but he'd fought his way in. If she pointed to it now, she would be well and truly raising the portcullis. Saying, *You are trusted here.*

And even though it was Mack—even though he was the one person in whose safe she would keep the key to her castle—it was still so hard to do. She wouldn't ever have thought to keep that key in his *hands.* They were too warm for the key to her castle. To her heart.

She took a deep breath, and then another.

And then she found his hand and squeezed it tight and lifted their joined hands together to indicate her bedroom.

Chapter 13

But they didn't quite make it. Nerves and awkwardness built in her again as they climbed the outside stairs to the upper porch, until she flinched a little when Mack, below her on the stairs, let his hand glide down her spine and brush over her bottom.

He caught her back to him suddenly as they stepped onto the porch. "Dance with me?"

The light she'd left on because she hated coming home to a dark house spilled gently over them, and the moonlight gilded the sea below. "Really?" If Prince Charming had just taken her hand at the ball, she would have been less surprised. Because, after all, who wanted to lower herself to some prince? No matter how handsome and charming he was, his asking her to dance would have been less perfect.

Mack found her remote on the old farmhouse craft table just inside the glass doors and turned on her music system. Anne started to smile, even as her eyes felt all shimmering like the sea.

It made her smile even more that he didn't choose a slow dance. No, this was real dance music. Not too fast, but a song to which he could spin her out and bring her back in.

"I would love to," she said.

"I've always loved to dance with you," he said as he brought her into him with a firm arm.

Her heart brightened. All this time, she'd assumed he danced so willingly with her for her sake and not his. As one of his easy gestures to make her happy.

"It always seemed like a special gift. That you would let me control you. That you'd trust me, when I did this." A swirl into a dip, easy and strong. His eyes held hers, serious but alight. Moonlight-on-deep-ocean happy.

"Well." Her breath caught in her throat and then released in slow pleasure as he righted her smoothly and spun her away. "You wouldn't let me fall."

"No, I wouldn't, Anne. Not if there was anything in this world I could do to help it." He wound her into him backwards, so that their arms crossed over her middle and her back was to his chest. His mouth brushed her temple.

A little smile ran through her, a curl of sweetness. "And you can do most things in this world," she allowed.

"I've never been able to do enough." He kissed her nape and lifted their arms, twisting her back around to face him. "The world's gotten through me three times now. It got to you."

"Fuck it," she said, and tried to make a fist to punch it in the nose, but of course her fingers were curled around his.

"God, I love how strong you are." He bent her back again, a long, slow tango dip. "You have no idea how erotic and gorgeous you are, when you're being strong." He kissed her throat, arched for him by the dip, and lingered there a moment, as if the position took no strength to hold at all. She gripped his shoulder, pulling herself up into him a little, giving him more access to her throat.

"What—what about when I'm being weak?" she gasped, because she felt all pliant right now.

"Then I want to be your strength." He pulled her upright and into him, this constant, flowing flex of power controlling her body. "And suck away your tears. And know that you'll be strong again one day. You've been my strength."

He spun her out and wound her in with a tug of his hand, until she was wrapped up tight against his body again, back to chest.

"We all have bad dreams in the night sometimes, Anne," he murmured to her ear. "I'd love to be here when you wake from yours."

Her hands shifted to clasp both of his to her, holding herself in tight in his arms. "Me, too." She realized it so suddenly. "Me, too. I want to be here for yours."

She never, ever wanted him to wake in the night alone when the experiences of his life tore at him again.

God. She could *be* there for him the next time something hurt him. Not waiting anxiously for her walk on the beach to see if he was getting through okay. She could be there in the dark. She could reach out and touch his face, his hand. She only had to let down her walls.

Only.

But they were *her* walls. She could do this. She could let him in. She *could.*

"Well, we're all right here, then." Mack's deep voice sounded so gentle and exultant both at once. "All the rest, learning how to sleep together, learning to feel comfortable with someone else seeing us at our silliest— drooling on a pillow, hair sticking up—that's all just habit, sweetheart. You can make me a new habit."

She twisted into him, breaking his control of the dance, to which he immediately adjusted, to yield to her way. He always did adapt when she sought control. "I want to." She held their hands tightly between them. "I really want to." *I still might need help. But I want this, too.*

"Then I've got everything I need, right here," he said, and snugged her in close. "Because what you want to do, you find a way to do."

"Not always," she said, with that bittersweet twist. Just as it had with him, the world had beaten her a time or four. Two miscarriages. A divorce. Trial and prison. The three little grandkids that had never come to be had hurt her terribly, too, this defeated grief. *Damn you, God. Not even granddaughters?*

Damn you. How dare you hurt my son?

"Yeah, but this time you've got me to help." Mack nudged her backwards into the house, still dancing, but closer in now, putting some dirty into it.

He turned out the lights she had left on inside as they went, leaving them in the glow of the nightlight peeking from the door of the bathroom and the moonlight from the veiled window. Funny how much sweeter it was to come home to a dark house with another person than to a lit house by herself.

It was chilly now, with the windows still open. But he held her in close, like a man who planned to keep her warm.

"You know what I'd like, right now?" he asked, in that ground-up voice close to her ear, a brush of warmth. And lower still, all the way down to a secret, just for her: "I'd like to feel you orgasm, under my hand. You have no idea how freaking beautiful that is." The bed brushed the backs of her knees. He lowered her, tango-slow and steady, as if it was just another dip in a dance. His voice was hushed as he repeated his words from just a moment ago: "It seems like a special gift. That you would let me control you. That you'd trust me, when I do this."

As her weight rested against the mattress, his hand trailed lightly over one breast, down her stomach, to rest—just rest, no pressure—against the juncture of her thighs.

She drew a slow breath in and out, controlling the instinct to cross her thigh over, to knock his hand away before he could make her that vulnerable.

She was already vulnerable to him. He had her. He'd had her forever. She just had to accept it.

"Or when I do this." He stretched out beside and above her, braced on one elbow, his other hand starting to rub oh-so-lightly at that point between her thighs. Not invasive. Barely enough pressure to be felt through her skirt. "Look at you," he said wonderingly. "Under me. Right here. Mine. I don't think I ever had enough trust in us for this fantasy, Anne. And I have to say—it's gorgeous."

She licked her lips and lifted herself a little to his hand. Just—that pressure. That warmth. Her skirt was too thick. Damn quality fabric and pencil form. She wanted it to be flimsy and flower-child swirly, something he could bunch up, something that didn't even stop his hand if he wanted to slide it between her thighs, and cup, and press.

His shirt had come half unbuttoned in the hammock. She pulled at it, sliding her hands to get at his chest, his body hard and warm and alive under her hands.

"I should have done this so long ago, Anne. I just—I never thought you'd let me. And I didn't want to break what we had."

"You said that was unbreakable," she reminded him. A little anxiety wanted to curl in her, at even the hint that it might be, but that anxiety couldn't manage the curl, because—well, it wasn't breakable. Even now, if they put an end to this deeper intimacy, they'd find their balance again and still have their friendship.

"It took me a long time to believe that, though," Mack said. "Most things in the world can be broken."

And that was when she realized something. "Me going to prison taught you some things, too, didn't it?" About her strength. About their strength.

"God, yes." He kissed her, urgent and angry, a hint of rage from just the mention of her going to prison. "It taught me how much I loved you, for one. It taught me that you could break my goddamn heart just as much as Julie or Jaime could. And it taught me that I'd damn well better grab you. Shit." He twisted his head away from her mouth to bite at her shoulder, as if the fierceness of his emotions had surged too high for her tender lips.

Then he nipped it again. And then he pushed her shirt aside, popping buttons again, and just ran his hand over her shoulder a moment, absorbed, tender, thorough. As if her shoulder was an amazing thing. "It taught me how strong you were." The one lesson she had guessed. "It taught me how much you matter. And I always thought I *knew* how much you mattered. But you mattered even more than that."

"I think I've always known how much you matter," Anne said. "And I think, at the same time, I'm still learning it more and more right now."

A flicker across his face of pleasure, of something more intense than both, and then he kissed her again.

Kissed down the line of her throat, over her shoulder, down the swell of her breast, pulling aside her shirt, undoing some buttons and popping others. "I love your taste in lingerie," he breathed against the golden-beige silk and subtle lace. "It's like kissing champagne."

She had this vision of herself going to his head, bubbling through him, making him giddy. It made her—sparkle. All through her, everywhere inside. It made her stretch to let all those sparkles slide freely from her fingertips to the roots of her hair to her toes. To her nipples and those surprisingly erogenous insides of her elbows, and dance its way on down, lower, deeper, more pleased with itself the lower and deeper it got.

"I like your taste in—nothing." She spread his shirt and stretched her fingers over the broad planes of his chest, with the curls of gray hair. "In just you."

"Yeah?" He leaned over her, lapping up the compliments and the stroking.

"Yeah," she whispered, tracing his muscles down over his ribs, hooking her thumbs possessively in his waistband as she curled her hands over his butt. "Yeah." *Mine.*

"I like your taste in nothing, too, but let me enjoy this pretty bra for a while. I didn't give it enough attention last time." He tongued her through the fine lace, sucking her into his mouth. That veiled intimacy worked so well on her. Instead of flinching back from her nakedness, she *wanted* it, wanted to have that veil fall away, so she could feel his mouth.

"Yeah," Mack breathed, scraping his jaw gently against her skin as he sought the other breast. "Like champagne."

Desire mounted in her, this hungry, confused thing. Desire could be tender? Could be starved and tender both? Her hands climbed up his back, under his shirt, the soft cotton panels falling to either side of her body.

"I must be getting drunk for real this time," Mack said. "Because I'm losing track of important things." One of his hands slid back down to that juncture between her thighs. "Like this."

She went still, breath coming in sips, as his heat soaked through her skirt again, so hot she could feel it through the layers of cloth. Such a frustrating protection, that cloth.

"You like that, don't you?" he breathed, deepening the rub of his hand just barely. Still the barrier was too thick, too much.

She closed her eyes, trying to concentrate on that elusive heat.

"Want to tell me what you want?" His thumb rubbed precisely, as if he knew exactly what she wanted, but those layers of cloth still blocked him.

She shook her head, her eyes still closed, chasing after that feeling.

"Want me to guess?" He found the edge of her skirt and stroked his hand under it, up her thigh, sure and warm and determined to reach his goal.

She nodded, eyes still closed. Her fingers kneaded into his shoulders and slid over his back, chasing sensations everywhere, as if she could drag them all in through her fingertips alone.

"I think you want me here." His hand pressed hot over her panties, and she shivered in relief at how much thinner they were than that skirt. *Now* she could feel him. Really feel him. She rocked herself against his hand involuntarily.

"I think you might even want me here." All the gravel was back in his voice, as his fingers dipped under the elastic of her panties and found her wetness. He made a low hum of approval, deep in his throat. "Oh, yes. Yes, I *like* how much you want me here."

She kept her eyes closed, focusing on him utterly. "I love your *scent*," she whispered. "I love the *warmth* of you. I love the expression in your eyes right now when I can't even see it. I love the way the panels of your shirt brush against my skin."

"Anne." His voice was wondering. His fingers dipped gently between the lips of her sex and stroked silk moisture upwards, finding her clitoris. "I have to get drunk on you more often. You say the damnedest things when I lose all inhibitions."

"Mack Corey." She twisted toward his fingers and shivered with pleasure, then shivered again when he responded to the first shiver by repeating the movement exactly. "You don't have inhibitions."

"You haven't been listening to what I've been saying, Anne. I've been holding back my fantasies about you for a long time. Just to make sure I kept what was most important."

She bit her own smile. "Me?" She kept her eyes closed, because she could see him better that way. See years and years of him, layered over each other, all compacted into the way he was looking at her right now. Such an intense way she had to veil it with her own eyelids.

"Exactly. Shh, now, sweetheart, you need to concentrate."

She did. He was so right, she did. All of her was focusing more and more on the sensation building under his fingers. That leisurely, steady rhythm, no hurry to get where he was going, no hurry to let *her* get there either. He was watching her. She knew he was watching her as he stretched it out, as he took his sweet time, watching every sigh and stretch of her body, every arch of her neck, every flicker of her eyebrows and working of her lips as she chased that feeling he kept drawing out.

"Mack." She grabbed at his hand.

"Well, you did tell me to guess." Another slow, savoring move of his thumb. "I like guessing. I like watching you and guessing every thing you want. Sometimes, in my fantasies, I like *not giving it to you*, so I can stretch it out." His fingers trailed away from her clitoris, playing with the lushness of her sex.

She made a frustrated noise and tightened her hold on his hand, fighting him for control of it.

"Shh, now, honey, you like this, too." His fingers dipped lazily deep into her and drew slowly out as his thumb played up and down her folds. "Don't you?"

"*Mack.*" Her muscles tightened around him. Her whole body bowed. But she needed—she had to have his thumb back higher. Back exactly where it had been. She dragged at his hand.

"That's the beauty of not being eighteen anymore, Anne. I just made love a few hours ago, and right now...I can take my time."

She reached immediately for his jeans, cupping him. Yes. They'd been dancing and making out, and she knew perfectly well he was aroused. He was trying to act as if he was all in control, but...she rubbed him, strong and sure, through his jeans.

"Mmm." A deep sound of pleasure.

"Want me to guess, too?" she challenged.

"Guess with them unzipped and your hand inside. I'll like that guessing game a lot better."

She let go of his hand to unbutton and unzip him, and, freed from her grip, his hand stroked a silky path back to that needy little nub and wet it with the moisture he had collected.

She lost all possible focus on his jeans, her hands halfway inside them, her body arching again as she lost herself to this sensation.

He pressed her hand hard against his erection and circled around her clitoris again. "Do you know in one of my favorite fantasies, I keep you like this all night?" he whispered.

Her eyes flew open at last.

His glittered, pitch black in the dimness. Funny, in her head, they had been blue. Vivid with light, like their walks on the beach in the early morning.

"Fortunately for you, my ability to imagine you begging for more of me all night only ever really lasted five minutes in the shower," he said wryly.

Oh, God, she wanted to take a shower with him. Be all slippery, and have his fingers act just...like...this.

"Mack." She bumped against him and tried to press his hand down.

"I know, honey. I can tell. All right, shh. Shh. Close your eyes again."

They fell closed of their own volition, pleasure vibrating through her again at the movement of his fingers. Oh, now he was serious. Now he was...clever, and...firm, and...insistent, and, and, and—

She just split apart. Fizzed out of herself like champagne, in this effervescence of being. Pleasure, pleasure, pleasure that he caressed and rode and caressed some more until she was almost crying, until she had to come down. She grabbed his hand and locked it between her thighs to hold it still, sobbing for breath. Subsiding. Subsiding. Slowly, slowly, slowly subsiding, a mad full-moon tide retreating at last.

"Shit, Anne," Mack said, very softly, and then shoved at his own jeans. "Do you mind if I'm, uh, in kind of a hurry?"

"Not eighteen," she managed to mumble, a ghost of teasing.

"Yeah, well. I told you how long my fantasies of all night actually lasted in my shower, didn't I? Jesus, Anne, you are *hot*." He got the condom on much more briskly than before, having apparently refreshed his memory of the process last time. He pulled her panties and skirt off both, in one swift movement, and braced himself above her. "Ready, honey?"

Oh, God, she liked the way he asked that. It sent this erotic charge of anticipation through her whole body. Like pausing at the top of a roller coaster, only the ride was going to be so much better. In answer, she wrapped her thighs around his hips and sank both hands into his butt, pulling their bodies together.

He groaned. And thrust into her, deep and hard.

She jerked with the pleasure of it. "God, that feels so *good*," she said incredulously.

She honestly hadn't remembered before that afternoon that a man's penis could feel that good inside her. Maybe because things had gotten so bad with Clark that sex had been this burden she tried to force herself through there at the end, but somehow, her associations with a man's penis had been ones of invasion, laboring, a little icky.

And the invasion was there, yes. Hell, yes, she was invaded. But, oh, God, all she wanted to do was get him to invade her *deeper*.

"Yeah," Mack said gutturally. "You're telling me. Oh, shit." He pulled out a little and thrust again, and then again. "Oh, yeah, do that, I like that," he urged as her fingers dug harder into his butt. "And you know how you squeezed on me earli—oh, *yeah*. God, Anne."

You're so damn easy, she thought on a wave of delighted tenderness, and squeezed again. Color flushed his cheekbones so deeply she could tell even in the moonlight. Or maybe she just knew that color was there from the heat of his skin.

"Anne," he begged. "Don't stop. Whatever you're doing, don't stop."

"I'm just lying here," she teased, stroking his butt. "Being me."

"Yeah. Don't stop that. Not ever." He thrust into her again. "Oh, God, not ever. Anne—"

She squeezed as hard as her inner muscles could, tightening her fingers on his ass.

He groaned and bent down suddenly, capturing her mouth in an utterly invasive kiss as his thrusts sped up. She kissed him back, giving him the savageness he asked for, sucking and yielding and invading in return as she arched her hips up to each thrust and squeezed with hands and thighs and all those inner muscles that were delighted to learn they had a purpose.

And she got to watch him, eyes wide open, as he came, body wrenching with pleasure, his own eyes closing, his body at last slowing and then hanging heavily from the arms still bracing it above her. He breathed in slow and huge and let it out as he slumped.

She stroked his back now, watching him. This was a nice order to things—he made her vulnerable first, exposed her all to him, but in return, she took him completely and made him hers. She'd never seen Mack Corey utterly yielded to any force in the world at all. And now here he was, yielded to her.

It was a long time before he rolled to his side, then went into the bathroom for a moment. When he came out, she watched him walk across the room, all naked now but still moving with that power in him. If he had to conquer the world naked, then he'd conquer it naked. And make everyone else feel pitiful hiding in their armor of business suits.

He slid into bed with her and tucked himself immediately against her, one arm going over her waist.

"I see I won't ever have to worry about lying there bored, wondering how much longer it's going to take you to get this over with," Anne couldn't resist teasing, pretending to glance at an invisible watch.

"Hey." He pretended to smack her on the bottom, then let his hand linger, a little rub of calluses over her roundness. "I'll have to tell you about my spanking fantasies sometime."

Her eyebrows shot up in indignation. He had better *not* have ever indulged in a spanking fantasy about her. "Only if I get to tell you about mine first," she said, and smacked *his* bottom, with a bit more firmness than he had hers.

Mack laughed and pulled her in closer. "I'm crazy in love with you, Anne. I don't know if I've ever mentioned that?" He rubbed his head into the pillow, a man ready to sleep for the night.

"I guessed," she said, and closed her fingers over his as they fell asleep.

Chapter 14

"Damn, I miss my girls." Mack sighed. He was gazing across the ocean, body angled slightly north, and while a sense of global orientation wasn't Anne's strongest suit, she suspected that if you could draw a line from his gaze and curve it across the Atlantic, you'd hit the Eiffel Tower.

Mack turned away from his line on Paris, one hand in his pocket, and took her hand with his other one. Even though Anne knew he must genuinely miss his girls terribly, happiness underlay his every movement. As if joy buoyed him up.

She looked down at their hands together. Her. She was that joy.

"About the sand thing," Mack said. "I could bring blankets."

"Have you ever had your genes scanned to see if somewhere back there your ancestors got crossed with a rabbit?"

He gave a shout of laughter. "It's just the build-up," he said plaintively. "I've been thinking about this for over a decade, and it's only been a week. You've got to let me work some things out."

"Maybe you should pace yourself." Anne's mouth twitched. "Considering you're not eighteen."

"Nah," Mack said instantly, shaking his head. "*Never* put off until tomorrow the hot sex you could be having today. You just never know what might happen." And his hand squeezed a little on hers, because under the humor they both knew that the world was like that. You really did never know.

She squeezed his back. *I'm right here, right now. That's the best I can do.*

Mack threw a stick for Lex, who bounded after it into the low morning surf. "With blankets, there'd be no reason for you to even touch the sand, let alone get it in the places you keep insisting it would get."

Yes, he was nothing if not persistent. "There are other houses on this beach, Mack."

"It would be the middle of the night! Most of these guys are old. At least, oh, forty. They'd probably be asleep."

"The neighbor two doors down has teenagers."

"Teenagers." He waved his hand. "They've probably got their headphones on, studying all night."

Yes, his concept of adolescent behavior might have been slightly warped by his daughters. Of course, *he'd* warped *them*, if they were so determined to impress their father that they studied all night when everyone else was playing video games. Still...warped or not, they seemed to be pretty happy, healthy, beautiful adults.

Her son, too. Who'd, ah, spent a lot of nights studying to be the best. Possibly, yes, to impress her.

"Mack. I am not getting my photo in the tabloids naked on the beach with you. No."

Lex came bounding back, shaking water, and Mack tugged on the stick with him, letting the dog play with it the way he liked to, then threw it out again. "I could buy a private island," he suggested.

Anne burst out laughing. "You could," she agreed. So could she, actually. She'd never redecorated a whole island. "But think of the upkeep."

Mack tugged her in to face him, using his hold on her hand like his personal leash, which he had a tendency to do. "I love it when you laugh like that. I don't know how to explain how much. It just—fills me up." And he made a gesture up his torso that started as a fist at belly level and spread, fingers stretching out as they rose through his chest.

Yes. You make me feel like a bottle of champagne, too. "I made you something," she said softly.

Some of the parts she'd had to have overnighted, some of them she'd gotten by pulling apart her own jewelry. But she'd finished it yesterday. She hadn't quite found the moment she was brave enough to offer it. It was a vulnerable gift.

Now, though. Now here on the beach with him, she could maybe put herself that far out there.

Especially—his face just brightened up so much. "Did you really?" And then, after a second, with a little blue sparkle of humor to ease her. "Handcuffs? A leash?"

She laughed and, on the laugh, could pull the little wrapped package out of her pocket. Her ribbon had gotten a little mussed from being carried in her various pockets since yesterday, and she adjusted it compulsively so that the wrapping would look perfect before she handed it to him. The presentation of a gift, after all, really mattered.

When she looked up from it, to hand it to him, so much tenderness and understanding filled his eyes that it still, after a week, nearly bowled her over. She'd seen that expression on his face before, she realized. Many, many times in all their friendship. But now he let the tenderness in it out in the open.

He touched her face as he took the package, feathering his fingertips along her hairline. Then he very carefully did not rip the package, respecting every fold.

By the time he had gotten to the box at the center, she had taken a step back. Regretting a little that she'd trained him so long ago not to rip open her presents as if the wrapping didn't matter.

Because she felt vulnerable again.

In the box lay a dark brown leather bracelet. Very masculine, she'd made it herself. Woven in its leather cords were five charms. First, on one side, an old porcelain bead with a flower pattern on it that came from a necklace Julie had once worn, that Mack had given her when they were in college. Cade had chosen it before she left, when Anne had explained to her what she wanted to do. It wasn't an expensive necklace, but apparently it was one that had held a lot of sentimental value for Julie, the very first present Mack had ever given her, picked up spontaneously on one of their early dates, and one the girls remembered her wearing a lot.

Talking to Cade had been—strange, as a conversation. Awkward, for Anne, to reveal something so intimate as what she was trying to do and what that meant about her and Cade's father, but then Cade had looked so *happy* that it had almost made Anne cry. Not only was she laughing more easily these days, but the damn tears seemed to be more ready to flow, too. That was what she got for letting Mack melt her.

Only how she was supposed to have kept him back, she didn't quite know. It wasn't as if she could have poured burning oil down on him from her ramparts. He might have gotten hurt.

Mack drew the leather bracelet out of the box and touched the flowered porcelain bead with his thumb, rolling it carefully.

Then two Murano glass beads, gold leaf within them adding its shine to the rich, vivid red of one and blue of the other. Jaime and Cade, their colors brilliant, just as Mack had said. His thumb rubbed slowly over those, savoring them.

Then an irregular, octahedral shape, pointy and obstreperous and refusing to harmonize, a beautiful old cream color. She'd had a bone carver who'd moved to the US from New Zealand make it, a man whose work she had featured once on her show. One side of the shape, the largest plane, was delicately carved with a stylized grinning face, just suggestive of a tiki carving. Or an old wise man who liked to mock the young ones.

And then...then...this was the one that had been so hard. That made her breath hurt in her chest, to affirm this about herself, that made her throat strangle and her nose sting, and then, then, when she finally got the courage to thread it onto the leather cord, made all the hairs on the nape of her neck shiver and release their shivering in one great rush down her back and through her body as she braided the strands together below it, weaving it securely in.

To even look through the glass beads and pick that one out as *her*: a beautiful glass, infused with light, little threads of gold in it, just this hint of gold, so that it seemed to glow. She'd tried her best to get exactly what he had described, for her. It had felt like wrenching her heart open, to agree that she was that beautiful.

The last bead on the bracelet, it framed his life with her and Julie.

"Anne." His thumb pressed down hard on it, and then his other hand jerked up toward his face, and she looked up to see that his eyes had turned red, that he was pressing his fingers across them and one of those fingers left a wet smear. "Goddammit, when did I turn into such a watering pot?" he swore, under his breath. And again: "Anne." Just her name.

And then: "*Shit.*" He had to shove another tear off his face. "Shit, you've got me all—oh, shit." He buried his face in his hands, the bracelet held tight in his fingers.

Anne didn't know what to do—she never entirely knew what to do when emotions got too much for him— and so she rested her hand on his waist, so he would know she was there, waiting.

He dropped one hand from his face and wrapped it around her waist, pulling her in hard against him. His other hand, still holding her gift, came up to cup her head, bracelet and all, so that he could press her in still tighter.

He didn't say anything for the longest time, just squeezed. Once in a while, it felt as if he was about to release her, and then his arms would tighten hard again and squeeze some more, rocking her.

And it was the stupidest thing. But while she was there, being squeezed so tightly, a little tear snuck out of her own eyes and trailed down her cheek.

Damn it, that man melted her.

"You spoiled my idea," Mack said finally, his voice all rough. "Jaime won't let me buy diamonds, and I know you would rather have something that an independent artist made anyway, so I was going to go shopping. Talk to some of the artists you've featured, try to figure out the best stones and design and all that. Put myself on there, all big and bossy and dominating so you couldn't pretend I wasn't there, and stones for Kurt and Kai, and, I thought..." His voice grew a little... *shy.* "Would you like my daughters, too? I thought you, you...might. Like them on there. Or...or maybe your own, that you lost. Or Kurt and Kai's. I wasn't sure. So I was still thinking about it."

One of her hands was against his chest, and from her position with her head pressed against him it was nearly all she could see—her bare wrist. Where a bracelet like that would go. Where five tiny stars could be woven between the larger, living stones, his honoring of both her loss and grief and the love she had still been given in her life despite it. "I can add your mother in," she whispered suddenly, softly. Maggie Corey had died before Anne ever met Mack, and he hadn't thought to mention her when he spoke of the bracelet, too focused on the present, but of course, his mother should be there.

His arms flexed on her, in agreement or thanks.

"I would like your daughters on mine, very much," she said.

"Ah, shit." He buried his face in her hair. "*Damn it.*" A surreptitious sniffle.

She wrapped her arms around his waist and squeezed him, and then she stood on tiptoe and kissed his throat.

He twisted his head to kiss her, and when she framed his face with her hands, it was damp under her fingers. She petted the wetness off him. Silly, over-emotional man. All that emotion in him for *her.*

It just wrapped itself around her heart and held it so tight and warm and hard.

Then he made her fasten the bracelet around his wrist, the man looking as foolishly happy as Lex bounding out of the water with his stick. And then somber, almost, so happy it turned him serious, and he wouldn't stop petting the bracelet. Throw a stick to Lex, run his fingers over the bracelet, take her hand again, a steady routine. While their routine could be varied by schedules and weather, often they walked an hour or even more together each morning they were at the beach. Sometimes they fell into pace with each other in the afternoons, too.

"You know, there are other places we could walk," Mack said abruptly.

Anne raised an eyebrow at him. The beach only ran up and down the coast. "You know this is the best direction, so we don't walk straight into the sun on our way back."

"No, I mean—" He cleared his throat. "Like Paris. It's a nice city for a walk."

Ah. Her mouth curved a little. "I do hear the Seine at night is nice." She'd been there with him, actually, but when Jaime was hurt, so it hadn't been the same at all. And she'd been there on her own. Which also hadn't been the same at all.

"It's nice if you have someone *with* you," Mack said. "If you're just over there because your daughters are busy dumping you for some idiot, arrogant chocolatiers, it's fucking lonely."

She squeezed his hand. "But we did agree you liked them."

"Some days less than others," he growled, kicking the sand.

She had never known she had so many instincts to cuddle a grumpy man. "I can take a trip to Paris. That would be nice."

It would be a little weird, actually, because it had been Julie's favorite city, and where the two of them went for their honeymoon. But if any city could handle two sets of lovers, Paris could. He'd asked her, which meant he wanted her there, making new memories with him.

"Well, maybe more than..." Mack hesitated, glowering at the sand as if it was his personal enemy. Which would be a pretty scary position for the sand to be in, actually. "I mean, I know how you like to take over spaces, and I have this ghastly, stupid penthouse there now, all glass and steel and some ferns. Nobody should have to live in that thing. But...I mean, it's *big*. So you could work with it. Although my dad will probably be there half the time, I should warn you."

"Maybe you should sell it and get a couple of human-size apartments that are in the same building. One for you, one for him. So you each have your space but he's not feeling lonely and abandoned." *Nor you.*

"I could probably buy the building," Mack allowed absently, and she bit back a smile. She'd actually grown up very middle-class, and sometimes the world she was in now still struck her funny bone in odd ways. "There are bound to be some nice apartments on the other floors, or ones you could help me turn into nice apartments. And that stupid penthouse could be turned into a great workspace. I mean it's practically got a studio kitchen already, you'd just have to modify it a bit for your show. It's got enough rooms that some of your people could even stay there while you have them in Paris, and—"

He looked up to meet Anne's stare.

He dropped her hand to shove his in his pockets and kicked the sand again. That poor sand was going to fuse into glass if he kept looking at it like that. "I know," he growled at the sand. "I know they want their freedom from me. I know that's why they went to some idiot country that acts snooty toward anyone who actually makes money. I got the message. But I just...I mean..." His scowl was so mighty. "When they start having my grandkids and everything, they might—"

He broke off, heaving a sigh, and bent his head and brooded. "I mean, if it's only for a few months a year," he burst out hopelessly. "Just another one of our bases, you know. That would be okay, right?"

Anne slipped her hand down into his pocket to find his. "Honey." It was the first time she had ever called him any endearment whatsoever, so she had to steal his for her. It felt odd in her mouth and sounded silly, but sometimes *Mack* was too crisp a word. "Your daughters love you. You know that, don't you?"

He swallowed and gave a wobbly movement of his head that was trying to be a firm nod but ended up not sure of itself.

"They're so happy to see you happy right now," she said. "I suppose they do need their independence. You're a really dominant man. But they love you." All those conversations she'd kept overhearing in the gardens, the two girls delightedly speculating on their father's love life.

She'd run into a similar conversation between Kurt and Kai, and it still soaked through her, that sweet, painful, beautiful reminder of what it meant: *He loves me, too. Even if I screwed some things up. He still loves me.*

Mack swallowed. "So...just a little bit?" He held up thumb and forefinger pinched close together. "Maybe a month around Christmas, a month in the spring, and...maybe a little more when Cade gets pregnant? Or Jaime." His face winced. "Jesus," he said very softly to himself. Clearly, he had barely started to adjust to the idea of his older daughter having kids, and imagining his younger pregnant was still a bit of a shock to his system.

"Maybe we should go over there when Summer has her baby, too," Anne said quietly. "I think that would really mean a lot to her."

Mack's face eased. "Good thought." He slipped his hand out of his pocket so that he could properly close it around hers again.

"After all, even her parents might show up for something like that, and you're about the only person who can take Sam on and run interference for Summer and the baby. Luc could, but he'll be sleep-deprived and he shouldn't have to deal with that shit while he's a new father."

Mack started to get that little smile on his face, the one that meant he was anticipating a battle. "Luc." He shrugged broad shoulders and made a tiny, dismissing gesture like an old, hardened warrior-king taking charge of a battle: *Step back, kids, and let me show you how it's done.* "Yeah, I'll handle Sam. Don't make an actual bath mat out of Mai or anything."

Anne made a face. Contact with Summer's mother always made her want to wash something sticky off the tips of her fingers. "I make no promises. Except to wear gloves, if I strangle her."

"Good thinking," Mack said absently. "And take the Fifth this time."

Anne rolled her eyes to heaven. Yes, *everybody* had ideas about how she could have handled that whole pursuit by the Justice Department better. Probably the price she paid for being loved by two strong, intelligent men who wanted to figure out every possible way they could prevent her from ever being caught in such a mess again.

Being loved. Having people who wanted to *save* her. She could probably handle a little annoyance as a price. If she could get past this damn eye-stinging, throat-strangling thing that happened whenever she thought about it.

"About the *we*," she said.

Mack's hand tightened hard on hers. "Damn it, don't start again, Anne. We've been dating for more than a decade. You can do this. Come on. Please?"

Aww. He had said please. For her.

She bent her head, concentrating on the feel of her hand in his, smiling foolishly at the sand. Poor sand probably needed someone to smile at it after all Mack's scowls.

"Are you sure this is what you really want?" Even as the words left her mouth, she knew how stupid they were, and Mack's incredulous look treated them as such.

"Anne. I run one of the top corporations in the world. Exactly how much mental energy do you think I have leftover to pursue things I'm not sure I want?"

"Well..." She opened her free hand. Okay, okay, it was a stupid question.

"You're hedging," he said severely. "*Again.* Damn it, Anne. Quit being a coward."

Her spine stiffened. "I beg your pardon?"

He closed his eyes a second. "Holy *crap*, you shouldn't give me that look when we're so far away from a house. Unless you want to reconsider your opinion about making love on a beach."

"We might discomfit the neighbor over there walking his dog," she said dryly.

"Anne. Quit beating around the bush."

"Well, what about Machu Picchu?" she said.

Mack stopped in the sand, staring at her blankly. "*What?*"

She gestured with her free hand. "Paris. The beach. Fine. That all suits you. What if I want to hike to Machu Picchu? Or Mount Kilimanjaro? Or...I've been working all my life, Mack. What about some of these other things?"

"Hey." His face lit up. "You want to hike to Machu Picchu, too? Seriously? I've been wanting to do that since I was a teenager, and I just never found the time. And then the girls weren't old enough, and then all the sudden they were teenagers who didn't want to do things with their dad. And then...I don't know. It didn't seem as much fun to do it by myself. But I never wanted to just cheat and take a helicopter up. That stole all the fun out of it."

"I think we should broaden our scope." She gestured again. "Not just limit ourselves to the beach."

"Anne Winters. That is *exactly* what I've been trying to tell you. You're just trying to twist it around to make it seem as if it was your idea. And you're splitting hairs to do it, I might add. You know damn well I'll hike whatever trail you ask me to."

Yeah. She did know that. She couldn't stop smiling at him.

He tightened his hold on her hand and lifted it between them, turning to face her. He couldn't stop smiling at her, either, this deep, intense, very serious smile. "Anne. Will you walk everywhere with me?"

She beamed at him. She couldn't help it. She felt like a damn lighthouse. "I will." Her voice choked up. She swallowed and took a breath, and her voice came out true and pure and clear. "If you'll walk everywhere with me."

His hand tightened on hers so hard. "Then we're good. Because I will."

She had to turn away, before she started getting as teary as he had. "I thought you might say that," she told the sand, with that foolish smile.

He took a long stride to catch up with her as she tried to head on, and ran his thumb under her eye. "Caught you," he whispered, showing her the gleam.

She drew a deep breath and lifted her chin, trying not to sniffle. "I'm just worried about whether you put the cap on the toothpaste. Because you know that one will be hard on me, if you don't."

He grinned. Actually, it was more like a sunrise, this joy bursting over the horizon. "Anne. I will even, even, even put the cap on the toothpaste for you."

She beamed, hugging herself with one arm, all of this silliness making everything feel so cozy, so real.

He bent to whisper in her ear. "I already did that anyway," he confessed. "Now breaking me of my other habits...we'll have to see. But you always did like a challenge, didn't you, Anne?"

She felt so smug. She felt like he looked, when he did that gloating *score* mark in the air. "Oh, yes," she said. "I always did."

He grinned. "Well, you've got one now, honey," he said, and locked his fingers tight with hers, swinging their hands as they headed down the beach.

She squeezed just as hard back and grinned up at him. "You, too."

***

THE END

THANK YOU!

Thank you so much for reading! If you have time to leave a review in your place of choice, these are hugely appreciated, and really help other readers discover books.

If you're interested in more, you can sign up to be emailed for new releases at http://lauraflorand.com/newsletter, or keep reading for glimpses of previously released books.

If you are interested in seeing more of Mack and Anne's children, you can find Jaime and Dom's story in *The Chocolate Touch*, Cade and Sylvain's in *The Chocolate Thief*, and Kurt and Kai's in *Snow-Kissed*. (Warning: *Snow-Kissed* was voted the AAR Tearjerker of the Year for a reason.) Luc and Summer's story is in *The Chocolate Heart*, and Patrick and Sarah's in *The Chocolate Temptation*. "Macaron Guy" Philippe's is in *The Chocolate Kiss*.

Keep reading for a complete book list and a glimpse of *Snow-Kissed* and *The Chocolate Touch*.

And feel free to join us on Facebook, where readers and I discuss books we're reading, chocolate we're tasting, macarons people are making, and other things that we have fun with. We'd love to see you there!

***

Website: http://lauraflorand.com/
Twitter: https://twitter.com/LauraFlorand
Facebook: http://facebook.com/LauraFlorandAuthor
Newsletter: http://lauraflorand.com/newsletter

OTHER BOOKS BY LAURA FLORAND

Snow Queen Duology
Snow-Kissed (a novella)
Sun-Kissed (also part of the Amour et Chocolat series)

Amour et Chocolat Series
All's Fair in Love and Chocolate, a novella in Kiss the Bride
The Chocolate Thief
The Chocolate Kiss
The Chocolate Rose (also part of La Vie en Roses series)
The Chocolate Touch
The Chocolate Heart
The Chocolate Temptation
Sun-Kissed (also a sequel to Snow-Kissed)

La Vie en Roses Series
Turning Up the Heat (a novella)
The Chocolate Rose (also part of the Amour et Chocolat series)
A Rose in Winter, a novella in No Place Like Home

Memoir
Blame It on Paris

SNOW-KISSED

The snow fell over the black granite counter in a soft hush of white. Kai focused on the sieve she shook as she brought a winter of sugar to the dark world, letting the powder slide across her thoughts the way snow on a falling night would, taking all with it, even her, leaving only peace.

That peace lay so cold. She had almost forgotten how cold she felt, until he showed up.

The man who, once upon a time, had always made her so warm and happy.

Now he stood at the window, looking as cold as she was. Destroying all peace. Past him and the pane of glass, only a few flakes fell against a gray sky, rare and disinterested, nature as usual failing her. Her fall of powdered sugar could not come between her and him, could not blur him to some distant place cut off by the arrival of winter. Could not hush him, if ever he chose to speak.

No, all she could do was concentrate on the sugar-snow. Looking up—looking at him—undid everything.

"I don't think they're coming," the man said finally, and she swallowed. It was funny how her whole body ached at his voice. As if her skin had gotten unused to his vibrations running over it. As if she needed to develop tiny calluses at the base of every hair follicle so that those hairs would not want to shiver.

Light brown hair neatly cut, he stood angled toward the window, shoulders straight, with that long, intellectual fitness he had, the over-intelligent, careful man who had played sports almost like he might study for a test, maintaining perfect physical fitness as just another one of his obligations. She still remembered when he had discovered Ultimate Frisbee, the awkward, unfamiliar, joy-filled freedom in him as he explored the

1

idea of playing something so intense *just for fun.* It had been rather beautiful. She had gone to all his games and chatted with the other wives with their damn babies and even played on his pick-up teams sometimes, although unwilling to put forth the effort to be part of his competitive leagues.

Those fun, fun years full of weekends of green grass, and friendly people, and laughter. They had had too many happy days. They clogged in her all the sudden, dammed up too tight, hurting her.

She had screwed them all the fuck up. Forever.

She didn't know what to say to him, after what she had done, so she concentrated on shedding snow, like some great, dangerous goddess bending over her granite world, a creature half-formed from winter clouds, drifting eerily apart from all humanity. She wished he had not come, but the thought of him leaving wrenched a hole in her that filled up instantly with tears.

Hot, liquid tears that sloshed around inside her and wanted to spill out. That in itself was terrifying and strange; she had thought she had tamed her tears down to something near-solid and quiescent, a slushy of grief that lay cold in her middle but no longer spilled out at every wrong movement, every careless glimpse of happy couples or children laughing in a park.

She had so hoped that she had reached a point where she could—see him. Where all that long process of coming to peace with herself and her losses would be strong enough to withstand a glimpse of him. But all of her, every iota of strength and peace, had dissolved into pain and longing the instant she saw him step out of his car, a flake of snow catching on his hair.

Damn it, his mother was supposed to be here. She was supposed to come with her magazine staff for this shoot, a whole entourage to make it easier on both Kai and Kurt. How could they have abandoned her to this reopening of wounds because they were afraid of a few flakes of snow?

2

She focused with all her strength. She had to get this sugar exactly right, not too thick, not too shallow, not too even, not too ragged, leaving perfect graceful curves and fades into black at its edges. It was soothing to work on that white against gleaming black. To focus on those tiny grains, almost as tiny as cells of life.

She could control these grains. She could always get them right. If she worked hard enough. If she really, really tried.

"The snow is supposed to start from the south and close us off," Kurt said from the window. "They probably didn't want to chance it."

Now why would Anne Winters's staff do that to her? Leave her alone with him just to avoid bad roads? Those selfish people, it was almost as if they had . . . families. Reasons to live that were far more important than she was.

Kurt shifted enough to watch her, but she didn't look up. She shouldn't have let him come, but for God's sake, his mother was Anne Winters. First of all, Anne had only rented the cabin to Kai so affordably on the condition that Kai maintain it for her use in photo shoots when she wanted it. And even without that agreement, Kai was a food stylist who regularly contracted to Anne Winters's company. She could hardly refuse this photo shoot for next year's holiday edition, Anne's biggest. And accepting it, she had to jump through Anne's hoops, even the famous multi-tasker's insistence on having her lawyer son with her for the weekend so she could work on contract negotiations simultaneously. Her formidable presence and the bustle of her staff should have helped dissipate all this miasma from their past and saved them from any need to linger in it.

Besides, Kai was supposed to be strong enough for this now. She had worked so hard to heal, to grow strong. To still and chill those tears down to something— bearable.

"Are you ready to be snowed in?" Kurt asked. "Do you want me to run to the store and pick up any supplies while there's still a chance?"

Her stomach tightened as if he had just pierced it with some long, strange, beautiful shard of ice. *Kurt. Don't take care of me. You always did that so, so*—the ice shard slid slowly through her inner organs, slicing, hurting—*well.*

"Why don't you check your email so that you'll know for sure whether they've cancelled?" he suggested. "Or find your charger so I can check my phone?" They had matching smartphones; their shared two-year contract still hadn't expired.

She didn't check her email or find her charger mostly because she didn't dare leave this powdered sugar snow. She had to keep her focus. She had to.

She hadn't yet managed to say a word to him. When she had opened the door, she had meant to. It shouldn't have been so hard. *Hello, Kurt.* She could say that, right? After practicing it over and over in her head on the way to the door. But the instant their eyes met, his hazel gaze had struck her mute. As the moment drew out, his hand had clenched around his duffle until his knuckles showed white, and his whole body leaned just an inch forward, as it had so many, many times in their lives, when she greeted him after a long day or a trip, and he leaned in to kiss her.

She had flinched back so hard that her elbows had rapped the foyer wall with a resounding smack, and he had looked away from her and walked quickly into the cabin without speaking, disappearing to find a room for his things. It had been at least twenty minutes before he reappeared, his hands in his pockets, to set himself at that post by the window and watch the road. Probably sending out a desperate mental call to his mother: *Hurry up, God damn it. Where the hell are you?*

But the cars hadn't come, and now he watched her. She could feel his gaze trying to penetrate her concentration on the snow. But she had to get that powdered sugar snow just right. She had to. Even if she had to play at snow for all eternity.

"Kai," he said and she shivered. Her name. Her name in his voice. "Can you still not even look at me?"

Named one of the best books of 2013 by Dear Author and Romance Novels for Feminists, #1 in Amazon's Short Fiction, and voted by readers as the AAR Tearjerker of the Year (you are warned). Available now!

THE CHOCOLATE TOUCH

" She's back."

Dom straightened from the enormous block of chocolate he was creating, gave his *maîtresse de salle,* Guillemette, a disgruntled look for having realized he would want to know that, and slipped around to the spot in the glass walls where he could get the best view of the *salle* below. He curled his fingers into his palms so he wouldn't press his chocolaty hands to the glass and leave a stain like a kid outside a candy shop.

She sat alone as she always did, at one of the small tables. For a week now, she had come twice a day. Once in the morning, once in the afternoon. She was probably a tourist, soaking up as much French artisanal chocolate as she could in her short stay in Paris, as they liked to do. But even he admitted it was strange that her soaking up should be only of him. Most wandered: him in the morning, Philippe Lyonnais in the afternoon, Sylvain Marquis the next day. Tourists read guidebooks and visited the top ten; they didn't have the informed taste to know that Sylvain Marquis was boring and Dominique Richard was the only man a woman's tongue could get truly excited about.

This woman—looked hard to excite. She seemed so pulled in on herself, so utterly quiet and contained. She had a wide, soft poet's mouth and long-lashed eyes whose color he couldn't tell from that far away. Hair that was always hidden by a hood, or occasionally a fashionable hat and a loosely tied scarf, like Audrey Hepburn. High cheekbones that needed more flesh on them. A dust-powder of freckles covered her face, so many they blurred together.

The first day, she had looked all skin and bones. Like a model, but she was too small and too freckled, so maybe just another city anorexic. When she had ordered a cup of *chocolat chaud* and a chocolate éclair, he had

1

expected to see her dashing to the *toilettes* soon after, to throw it up before the binge of calories could infect her, and it had pissed him off, because he loathed having his chocolate treated that way.

But she had just sat there, her eyes half closed, her hands curling around the hot cup of chocolate caressingly. She had sat there a long time, working her way through both éclair and *chocolat chaud* bit by little bit. And never once had she pulled out a journal or a phone or done anything except sit quite still, absorbing.

When she had left, he had been surprised to feel part of himself walk out with her. From the long casement windows, he had watched her disappear down the street, walking carefully, as if the sidewalk might rise up and bite her if she didn't.

That afternoon, she was back, her hands curling once again around a cup of his *chocolat chaud*, and this time she tried a slice of his most famous *gâteau*. Taking slow, tiny mouthfuls, absorbing everything around her.

Absorbing him. Everything in this place was him. The rough, revealed stone of the archways and three of the walls. The heavy red velvet curtains that satisfied a hunger in him with their rich, passionate opulence. The rosebud-embossed white wall that formed a backdrop to her, although no one could understand what part of him it came from. The gleaming, severe, cutting-edge displays. The flats of minuscule square chocolates, dark and rich and printed with whimsical elusive designs, displayed in frames of metal; the select collection of pastries, his *gâteaux au chocolat*, his éclairs, his *tartes*; clear columns of his caramels. Even the people around her at other tables were his. While they were in his shop, he owned them, although they thought they were buying him.

The third afternoon, when the waiter came upstairs with her order, Dom shook his head suddenly. "Give her this." He handed Thierry the lemon-thyme-chocolate éclair he had been inventing that morning.

He watched the waiter murmur to her when he brought it, watched her head lift as she looked around. But she didn't know to look up for him and maybe didn't know what he looked like, even if she did catch sight of him.

When she left, Thierry, the waiter, brought him the receipt she had left on the table. On the back she had written, *Merci beaucoup*, and signed it with a scrawled initial. L? J? S? It could be anything.

A sudden dread seized him that *Merci* meant *Adieu* and he wouldn't see her again, her flight was leaving, she was packing her bags full of souvenirs. She had even left with a box of his chocolates. For the plane ride. It left a hole in him all night, the thought of how his *salon* would be without her.

But the next morning, she was back, sitting quietly, as if being there brought repose to her very soul.

He felt hard-edged just looking at her restfulness, the bones showing in her wrists. He felt if he got too close to her, he would bump into her and break her. What the hell business did he have to stand up there and look at her? She needed to be in Sylvain's place, somewhere glossy and sweet, not in his, where his chocolate was so dark you felt the edge of it on your tongue.

She needed, almost certainly, a prince, not someone who had spent the first six years of his working life, from twelve to eighteen, in a ghastly abattoir, hacking great bloody hunks of meat off bones with hands that had grown massive and ugly from the work, his soul that had grown ugly from it, too. He had mastered the dark space in his life, but he most surely did not need to let her anywhere near it. He did not like to think what might happen if he ever let it slip its leash.

"She certainly has a thing for you, doesn't she?" his short, spiky-haired chocolatier Célie said, squeezing her boss into the corner so she could get a better look. Dom sent a dark glance down at the tufted brown head. He didn't know why his team persisted in treating him like their big brother or perhaps even their indulgent father, when he was only a few years older than they were and would be lousy at both roles. No other top chef in the whole city had a team that treated him that way. Maybe he had a knack for hiring idiots.

Maybe he needed to train them to be in abject terror of him or at least respect him, instead of just training them how to do a damn good job. He only liked his equals to be terrified of him, though. The thought of someone vulnerable to him being terrified made him sick to his stomach.

"She must be in a hotel nearby," he said. That was all. Right?

"Well, she's not eating much else in Paris, not as thin as she is." Célie wasn't fat by any means, but she was slightly more rounded than the Parisian ideal, and judgmental of women who starved themselves for fashion. "She's stuck on you."

Dom struggled manfully to subdue a flush. He couldn't say why, but he liked, quite extraordinarily, the idea of Freckled Would-be Audrey Hepburn being stuck on him.

"You haven't seen her run throw anything up?" Célie checked doubtfully.

"*No,* she doesn't—*non.* She *likes* having me inside her."

Célie made an odd gurgling sound and looked up at him with her eyes alight, and Dom replayed what he had just said. "Will you get out of my space? Don't you have work to do?"

"Probably about as much as you." Célie grinned smugly, not budging.

Hardly. Nobody worked as hard as the owner. What the hell did Sylvain Marquis and Philippe Lyonnais do with employees who persisted in walking all over them? How did this happen to him? *He* was the biggest, ugliest customer in the whole world of Parisian chocolate, and yet in his own *laboratoire*—this was what he had to put up with.

Célie waggled her eyebrows at him. "So what's wrong with you? Are you sick? Why haven't you gone up with your—" She braced her shoulders and swung them back and forth, apparently trying to look macho and aggressive. She looked ridiculous. "We could cover for you for a couple of hours."

She tried to treat it like a joke, the way Dom could walk up to a woman, his aggression coming off him in hard edges all over the place, and have that woman get up and disappear with him for a couple of hours. But a profound disapproval lurked in her brown eyes.

Dom set his jaw. His sex life was really *nobody*'s business, even if it was infamous, and, well—"*No*. Go start on the *pralinés* before I make you come in at three a.m. tomorrow to do them."

For a wonder, Célie actually started to move. She got three steps away before she turned back. "You haven't had sex with her already, have you? Finally broken someone's heart, and now she's lurking here like a ghost, snatching at your crumbs?"

Dominique stared at her. "Broken her—ghost—crumbs—what the *hell* do you guys make up about me when I'm not in earshot?" He never had sex with women who had hearts. Not ones that beat for him, anyway.

"Nothing. We contemplate possible outcomes of your actions, *chef*, but I think we're pretty realistic about it." Célie gave him her puckish grin and strolled a couple more paces away. Naturally, his breath of relief was premature, and she turned back for one last shot. "Now if we were *creative*, we might have come up with this scenario." She waved a hand at Dom, wedged in a corner between glass and stone, gazing down into his *salle* below.

Whatever the hell that meant.

He blocked Célie's face from the edge of his vision with a shift of one muscled shoulder and focused back on the freckled *inconnue*'s table.

Merde, she had left.

Available now!

ABOUT LAURA FLORAND

Laura Florand was born in Georgia, but the travel bug bit her early. After a Fulbright year in Tahiti, a semester in Spain, and backpacking everywhere from New Zealand to Greece, she ended up living in Paris, where she met and married her own handsome Frenchman. She is now a lecturer at Duke University and very dedicated to her research into French chocolate. For some behind the scenes glimpses of that research, please visit her website and blog at http://lauraflorand.com. You can also join the conversation on Facebook at http://facebook.com/LauraFlorandAuthor or email Laura at laura@lauraflorand.com.

COPYRIGHT

CPSIA information can be obtained at www.ICGtesting.com
Printed in the USA
LVOW11s0340090914

403157LV00002B/85/P